Nightwalker

Louis Bruno

No Ceiling Books—Walnut Creek, CA
ISBN: 979-8-9896728-2-0
eBook ISBN: 979-8-9896728-5-1
Library of Congress Control Number: 2023923476
Title: *Nightwalker*
Author: Louis Bruno
Digital distribution | 2024
Paperback | 2024

Dedication

iii

To my parents, who planted the seed of knowledge in my mind, nurtured it and believed in me.

To my wife, my true love, best friend and most profound inspiration.

To my daughters, who fill my heart with joy, encourage me and make me endlessly proud.

To Andrew, for his brilliant cover design, wonderful creativity, support, friendship and love.

To all those who may pick up this book, thank you for giving my words a chance.

Chapter 1

Nick Malloy stared into the cool October night. He could see his own breath as he exhaled. A fleeting, misty cloud. The temperature was dropping. He put his hands into the pockets of his long, black leather coat and hiked up the collar. A cigarette dangled from his mouth, bobbing up and down as he mumbled to himself. Following one last long inhale, he flicked the butt to the cement and stomped it with his high-top sneaker.

Nick was in his thirties, with long and slender facial features. His build was lean but wiry. His thinning brown hair was pulled back into a ponytail, and he had a perpetual three-day stubble. He repeatedly checked the time on his cell phone. Almost 9:30 p.m. *Where is this guy?* Patience wasn't his strongest attribute. He twirled his pen and tapped his foot with a rhythmic flow, blowing air out of his cheeks.

Just as he was about to leave, he heard footsteps and glanced sideways. Nick grinned when he saw Minnesota approaching. That was the nickname he'd given to one of his most loyal customers. Pudgy with a blonde crew cut, matching goatee, sky-blue eyes, and about five years removed from high school. Minnesota had been introduced to Nick at a party over a year ago. They didn't exchange Christmas cards, but the two maintained a civil and steady buyer-seller relationship.

Minnesota narrowed his eyes. "Why do we always meet out here, Nick?"

"Where would you prefer, behind Dunkin' with cop cars all over the place? The boarded-up supermarket and the woods give us privacy. I like to think of it as my little office, my home away from home."

"There's only one streetlight in this area and it's out."

Nick pressed his lips together. "I'll place a work-order request with Con Edison tomorrow. Can we move this along? You were late and I have other customers."

"Okay. How much?"

"$20."

Minnesota raised his eyebrows. "A Jackson! Nick, help a guy out. I'm a regular. I only want a tenth of a gram. I'll need more by the end of the week. Give me a break?"

Nick wore a fake smile. "This isn't Walmart, and I don't hand out rewards cards. The gangs around here will sell it to you for double my price, and you're lucky if you make it back to your car alive. This heroin is pure, from Columbia. It's not cut with fentanyl. No additives. No blends. Who looks out for you?"

Minnesota let out an exasperated sigh. "Yeah, yeah, everybody looks out for me. Stop with the commercials."

"I'm telling you; this heroin's the real thing. Good as mother's milk." Nick heard a noise and turned sharply to his right. "Did you hear that?"

"Yeah. What do you think, cops?" Minnesota asked.

"Maybe your wife."

"I'd rather it be cops. Either way, I'm getting out of here. Here's the money."

Nick took the $20 bill and handed Minnesota a bag containing a tenth of a gram of heroin, who slipped it into his front pants pocket. "See you around." He then hustled away towards Queens Blvd., disappearing into the night.

Nick blew on his hands, then rubbed them together earnestly. He tugged at his jacket collar, ducking his head down a bit. He hadn't heard the sound again and figured it had been a squirrel scurrying through the wooded area behind the abandoned market.

Nick stared out in the direction his customer had travelled. He noticed a large yellow and red sign in the distance, hovering high above Queens Blvd., illuminating that area. It was the McDonald's Golden Arches, containing a billboard like proclamation. Billions and Billions served. It made him wonder how many customers he'd served. It certainly wasn't billions, but he did well.

The buzzing of his phone interrupted his inner business acumen discussion. "Hello. Hey, what's up? How much do you need? That much. Really partying tonight! You're looking at $500. Okay, I just finished up here. I can meet you at our usual spot in about 15 minutes. Good. See you then."

Another customer soon to be served.

A sudden sound, closer than the last one, made Nick recoil. Someone, or something was moving around nearby. He crouched down somewhat and took a step back, his breathing shallow and rapid. Nick's neck muscles stiffened, his deep-set eyes darted back and forth, and his phone was now resting in his clammy palm. He wondered who would win the battle being waged between his fight or flight response. This was the reason he wore sneakers for work-related meetings.

Was it cops? Competitors? An animal? Nick eliminated the idea that Publishers Clearing House had finally tracked him down. His spicy dinner was beginning to attack him, and he felt as if his heart was pumping a mixture of cayenne pepper and battery acid.

The darkness was making it difficult for Nick to determine what or who was out there. He squinted to try to make out an image as he glanced in the direction that another quiet sound emanated from.

With increased pitch in his voice, Nick asked, "Someone there?"

He never saw it coming, never heard it, and had no time to react. He had no opportunity to duck, yell or plead. A bullet slid past hair, skin, and muscle before smashing into his brain. Nick fell backwards to the ground, his hands limply resting at his sides, palms up, facing the clear autumnal sky.

The projectile entered and pushed its way through his prefrontal cortex. In the middle of his forehead, between his eyes, was a circular hole, rimmed with abraded skin.

Blood escaped profusely from the cavity in his forehead, sliding down his face, some making its way past his chin and onto his throat. Some pooled at top of his lip, just below his now scarlet red nostrils. The blood was simultaneously rushing from the back of Nick's head, seeping onto the sand and dew-soaked grass of the woods behind the supermarket parking lot.

Nick's blood pressure plummeted, and he stopped breathing, His catastrophic bleeding had sent his body into severe shock, making it impossible for oxygen to be delivered to his vital organs.

In just a fraction of a second, he was gone.

Chapter 2

Detective Joe Devlin slammed down the phone after ensuring that his lieutenant hung up first. The Commissioner had apparently pressured the Chief of Detectives, who leaned on Lieutenant Moss, who in turn admonished Devlin. The media was hounding the Police Department, demanding solutions to the current crisis. Early this morning they'd found another dead body in Queens. This was the tenth gun-shot victim found in the last ten months in the Corona section of New York City's largest borough. Beginning in January, one murder each month. The latest victim was killed behind a boarded-up supermarket, between a dumpster and a wooded area.

The public was outraged and scared, and it was beginning to roll downhill, collecting at the front of Joe's door. He took one last puff of his Marlboro and then snuffed it out in his ashtray.

Joe was medium height, soon to be fifty, with intense blue eyes, carrying a few extra pounds and the weight of the world on his strong shoulders. He wearily rubbed his moustache between his right thumb and index finger. His head then tilted down until it rested in his left hand, where he could feel his forehead and receding sandy-blonde hairline. He'd been with the police department for almost 26 years and enjoyed a reputation of being honest, tough, and clever. Joe was an exemplary investigator, closing an impressive amount of homicide cases. Even though he had been promoted, he thought and acted like the beat cop he was as a 24-year-old rookie patrolling the streets of Queens with his partner and mentor, Al Silvani.

Al retired a few years ago but followed Devlin's career carefully. They spoke frequently on the phone and saw each other on occasion. Joe would pick Al's brain regarding a case when felt he'd hit a wall. He had a hunch that he'd be speaking with Al very shortly.

Joe had been informed that the chief of detectives, Harry Brenner, would be at their precinct around 3:00 p.m. to hold a meeting. Devlin wasn't told the purpose of the meeting, but assumed it wasn't for the Secret Santa gift raffle.

Homicide in New York City was not exactly unheard of, but last night's shooting was another with no apparent motive and no physical evidence (except for a dead person with a bullet in the brain). Each victim had been shot one time in the head at close range. Joe had been at the crime scene for the previous nine shooting deaths, which were still open and unsolved cases, getting colder by the day.

Brenner had accompanied Joe to the last crime scene, and for the first time, the Detective proposed the idea that these deaths might not be independent acts but rather a pattern that somehow fit together - which might be the work of a serial killer. Joe had attempted to broach that subject after the fifth victim was discovered, but his thoughts were dismissed. Brenner hated the idea of panicking the public. Joe realized Harry was a first rate "Chief of D's", but he'd let his fear of scaring the public override what seemed increasingly obvious. Now there was no choice.

Joe began preparing for Brenner's visit, knowing that he would address the detectives as an entire unit first, but would follow up with a one-on-one meeting with Joe.

He reviewed the files on the prior nine murders, and then added the tenth to the pile. He felt baffled. Joe had sent to prison a wide array of murderers, gang bangers, street criminals, drug pushers and various other scum over his career. He had a gift, a sixth sense for seeing the truth among all the lies. This, in concert with his dogged determination and perseverance, was why he was viewed as a talented and successful detective. But these circumstances were different.

Lieutenant George Moss broke into Joe's thoughts. "Fill me in on what you have before you meet with Brenner." Moss twisted the wedding ring on his finger, a gesture Joe knew was the lieutenant's "tell." Joe assumed Moss had gotten a tongue lashing from Brenner. It was still morning, yet Moss' tie was undone, his jacket off and his sleeves rolled up.

"Ten murders. People with no clear connections. No obvious similarities. I can't figure out if they're all part of the same puzzle."

"We have to make those pieces fit," Moss said, standing over Joe's desk.

"I'm going to suggest that we proceed with the theory that there *is* a connection and a motive and begin our investigation from that perspective," said Joe. "The challenge will be to find the commonality between the victims or the circumstances surrounding the murders."

"Brenner told me that there didn't seem to be anything connecting the victims. We need to determine if they were targeted or if they were just in the wrong place at the wrong time." Moss stroked his chin between his thumb and index finger. "What we do know is that beginning with this year there's been one murder each month. The victims were killed between 9:00 p.m. and midnight, and their bodies were discovered in remote spots. What else have you learned, Joe?"

"No prints at any of the crime scenes. No spent cartridges. No DNA evidence. No physical evidence of any kind, and so far, no witnesses. Only blood belonging to the victims. The Medical Examiner told me that none of the bodies had been moved post-mortem, so the killer fires his weapon, the D.O.A. drops to the ground, and the perp leaves the scene."

Moss nodded. "Okay, you'd better not be late. We'll talk this afternoon."

Joe collected all his papers, documents and files and made

his way to the meeting with Harry Brenner. His only hope was that Brenner's unwillingness to make a scene would spare him an undressing before his fellow detectives. Joe *had* warned Brenner about this possibility five months ago. Joe could already hear the conversation he would need to have with his former partner following this little get-together.

While walking down the dreary hall Devlin thought of the photos of the victims. They brought back memories of the death of his son Thomas, who was killed eight years ago while walking home from school, two weeks before his thirteenth birthday. A junkie had attacked his son, beating and stabbing him to death. Those photos reminded him of Thomas's sixth grade picture, which he kept in his wallet, and of his son's framed Little League photo. The detective often wondered what his son would look like now. He lamented the idea that he and his wife, Patty, would never experience special moments like graduation, a wedding, or grandchildren. That they'd been robbed of witnessing Thomas' growth and maturation, of seeing their son navigate life, blossom into a man and choose a career, life path and life partner. As Joe thought of all of this, he began to sweat, get panicky, his heart racing.

That tragedy had nearly destroyed both his personal and professional life. But he and Patty had saved their marriage. Following a hiatus from the force, Joe had become an even more determined investigator.

Still, the closing of homicide cases couldn't eradicate his pain. He carried around a perpetual gut-wrenching, heart sinking feeling. Joe tried very hard to repress these feelings. However, each day some sadness and anger seeped through, and some days, they were accompanied by a desire for vengeance.

Chapter 3

James Bradley finished tying the laces of his brand-new Nike sneakers. Black with gray trim. As he stood up, he took a quick glance in his bedroom mirror to make sure his walking ensemble had panache. A long sleeve black Under Armour shirt, dark shorts and a black baseball hat gave his outfit a monochromatic, yet athletic look. He studied his frame for a moment longer and smiled. Not bad for a forty-five-year-old attorney. He was six feet tall and about 180 pounds, with strong facial features, short brown hair and deep brown eyes.

As this was a brisk October evening, it would already be dark when he stepped out of his house at 8:00 p.m. He enjoyed dressing sharply and neatly, as one never knows when an opportunity might present itself. Jim was always prepared for any situation, from the courtroom to the ballfield to his great passion, which was taking long walks every evening. His even temperament allowed him to laugh with his friends about his idiosyncrasies. Besides, everybody had some odd tendency. Jim learned to accept and embrace his perfectionism, even if it meant that he was less than spontaneous most of the time.

However, his obsessiveness had increased following his brother's murder six years ago. A drug addict had shot David Bradley in the heart during an attempted robbery. Jim's therapist had explained that he was trying to repress memories through compulsive behavior. Maybe true, but Jim had mixed feelings about his year in therapy. Dr. Lawrence was helpful to a degree, yet the process was painful. He found that meditation, controlling his breathing and walking were more helpful.

During his sessions, Jim would get jumpy. He told his doctor about how he experienced flashbacks and endured nightmares. "I have these crying spells, doc, and they wash up on me like giant waves." Sometimes during his sessions tears would run from the corners of Jim's eyes, glistening on his cheeks. Repression, ultimately, was easier for him than reliving David's death.

At this moment Jim didn't want his mind to wander to that subject, as it had dominated his life for half a decade; and he wasn't in the mood to re-visit the agony, the depression, and the suicidal thoughts.

He went downstairs to get a bottle of water to bring with him on his walk. He kissed his Rottweiler Anakin on top of his robust head and then ate a granola bar. This was his nightly ritual. The only deviation was on some occasions Jim would give a second kiss to Anakin, his constant companion since David's demise. As a bachelor, his time was his own. But he'd gotten into a rut, eating high carb dinners with nothing to show for it but a potbelly and high cholesterol.

A slightly damaged right knee from his baseball playing days had made jogging impossible, so Jim began walking. Just a couple of times a week for about a half-mile at first. But as he began to revel in the tranquility of having the evening streets to himself, seeing his weight come off in concert with a healthier diet, the habit became more frequent with longer duration. Eventually he was able to go for hours if he wanted, enjoying the serenity of each mile, a stark contrast to the hustle and bustle of his New York City law firm.

There was a cool autumn breeze and accompanying pre-Halloween feel in the air. Jim was at the point where he was almost oblivious to the weather. Though he preferred the September through November months, he sojourned anytime of the year, from the extreme oppressive August heat to the frigid blustery February frost. Christmastime was the most festive, and Jim loved studying the houses lit up with beautiful holiday magic as he passed by.

As Jim was feeling in a particularly affectionate mood this evening, he dropped a second kiss on Anakin, who gave an approving lick to Jim's cheek. Unfortunately, many of the people in Jim's life did not share the traits Anakin displayed, loyalty, fearlessness, companionship and unconditional love.

The dog went to his usual resting spot, a comfortable animal bed between the fireplace and the big screen TV, watching Jim stroll to the door and then disappear outside. On some occasions Jim brought Anakin along, but tonight he would stroll solo. His guilt was assuaged because he paid for a daily dog walker so that his canine companion got a good workout while he was at the office.

As Jim stepped onto his porch, the crisp air hit him squarely in the jaw. The air was crisp and clean. A few stars glimmered in the late twilight sky. The moon was full.

His walks had become a psychological necessity for Jim, a way to try to rid himself of sorrow over his brother's death. Every night, he tried to overcome his grief, and every night, despite the respite of his walks, he failed. Maybe tonight he would finally "walk off" his sorrow.

Chapter 4

Jim's alarm sounded at 6:00 a.m. the next morning, waking both he and Anakin out of a sound sleep. He'd hoped that, by his age, his bed would be shared by an individual with blonder hair, longer legs, and much better breath. However, he'd accepted that beggars couldn't be choosers, and in the world of romance, Jim had fallen into the beggar category. As soon as his feet hit the floor, he thought how he'd give anything for this to be Saturday morning. Unfortunately, it was Monday and the beginning of another long week full of commuting, the office, and the courtroom, mixed in with the usual large helping of B.S. Instead of playing the *What would have happened if I took a different career path game* with himself, he made his way downstairs for breakfast, Anakin by his side.

Jim had grown tired of lawyering and the court game. For twenty years he'd been a very small cog in a big litigious machine, and now his parts had become warn and frayed. He longed for a change in his life, an epic one, but he was lost as to which path to pursue. His indecision only served to exacerbate his almost daily sadness. He was very tired, but not the type of tired that extra sleep could cure.

After Anakin had been fed and let outside, Jim scarfed down some scrambled eggs with toast and devoured two cups of coffee. He needed the caffeine both to wake up and to face his boss for another morning meeting to cover the weekly agenda. About nine years ago, Jim had become a junior partner at White & Dunn, a small firm in Midtown Manhattan that specialized in personal injury cases. What they didn't teach him in law school was that along with the money and status, partnership also ushered in a never ending array of issues such as inter-personal problems among the associates, who would all sacrifice their mother for a shot at advancement, constant criticism from the senior partners, all of whom dreaded the idea of losing their cushy positions and offices to the junior partners, and clients who assumed that if their barber took too much off the top they were entitled to damages.

Jim now dreaded going to work each day, a far cry from the enthusiasm and energy he had fifteen years ago when he began as an associate at the firm. He became a non-equity partner after his sixth year but had never been promoted to equity partner status. Even though his bitterness at this fate had subsided, he couldn't shake the lingering feeling that he was stuck in neutral. Yet, his current employment status was only partially responsible for the ennui he felt toward life in general. This discontent began six years ago following his brother's murder. Although time might heal most wounds, it couldn't heal them all.

The 7:35 a.m. train to Penn Station was packed this morning, as usual. Jim found a seat next to a large man and scrunched in next to him. The Long Island Railroad was a world onto itself. Shuttling people day after day to New York City and back. Commuters packed into these trains to avoid the heavy traffic that would greet them if they chose to drive into Manhattan. If lucky enough, Jim would have just enough energy left to collapse into bed on Friday night.

Jim entered the lobby of his building and stopped for a cup of coffee, a bottle of water and a newspaper, his usual order. He said hello to Raymond, the proprietor of the small store called *Coffee to go,* which been in the same spot throughout Jim's tenure at the firm. The two had become very friendly, and would discuss politics, sports and women, and although they'd agree that neither knew that much about any of these subjects, especially women, they could still pontificate with the best of them.

This morning Raymond was more interested in Jim's thoughts on the headline staring out at them from today's issue of one of the local papers. *Serial Killer Claims Tenth Queens Body.*

"You see this, Mr. B?"

"I wouldn't believe everything you read, Ray. That rag sometimes pulls a hamstring backtracking."

"I hear you," Ray laughed, "but most of the stuff in the article came from the cops. Looks like the real thing. It's all my customers are talking about."

"I'm not going to panic yet, Ray. Let's wait until all the facts are in. We've been down this road before. If you could take a few minutes away from conducting your investigation, can I have a large coffee, light and very sweet?"

"Sure thing," Ray laughed. "Have a good day Mr. B."

"You too." Jim smiled, grabbed his coffee, then headed to the elevator.

He reached his office suite on the 16th floor. He walked through the law firm's glass doors and made his way down the hall to his office. Jim put his briefcase on the chair facing his desk, hung up his suit coat and plopped into his chair. In the middle of his desk was a stack of papers the size of the Empire State Building. He'd decided Friday to forego digging into this pile and wait for Monday to tackle it, but now he regretted his procrastination. He had a half an hour before his meeting with William J. Dunn, the managing partner to whom he reported.

Jim strolled into William Dunn's office at 10:00 a.m. on the dot, as he had every Monday. Dunn was in his early fifties with thinning sandy-colored hair and a lean physique. He wore glasses and a gray three-piece suit accompanied by a snowy white shirt and cobalt blue tie.

They began with the usual weekend summary and round up. Normally Jim and Bill would then discuss the upcoming trials, the status of various cases and on occasion would have a dialogue regarding staff goals, capacity planning, bringing in new cases and marketing the firm. Today Jim noticed the newspaper folded in the corner of Bill's desk upon entering the office but chose not to broach the subject.

"You're lucky you're not married, Jim."

"Why's that?"

"Exhibit A," Bill gestured toward the newspaper.

"Does your wife object to the photos of celebrities carrying their two-pound dogs in one hand and a ten-dollar coffee in the other?"

Bill chuckled. "I wish. It's these murders all around Queens. The possibility of a serial killer on the loose. Now my wife wants to move out of the area."

"But you already live out of the area, you're in Westchester."

"You don't have to explain it to me. Allison is from the Midwest. Most of her family is still there. This morning she mentioned that we should consider getting out of the tri-state area altogether."

"There's no escape from crime, Bill." Jim thought about Dr. Lawrence's aphorism, "A safe zone doesn't exist." In therapy, Dr. Lawrence had instructed Jim that he could get past his fear and anger by meditating, breathing and walking. Even medication, which Jim tried but halted as his mind became foggy and his memory began to erode. So, his insecurity, sadness, anger and anxiety gnawed at him and made him feel trapped. Only walking helped.

"You're right. Try telling Allison, though. Anyway, let's get down to business."

Their discussion ended with a quick review of the agenda for the week and a promise to have lunch together on Wednesday. They shook hands as if to signify the signing of a treaty, and Jim hustled back to his office to begin preparing for his afternoon court appearance.

Jim enjoyed his interaction with William Dunn, even though his boss wasn't exactly 100 percent in the laughs department. His idea of creating a fun and light-working atmosphere was to put dimes in his penny loafers. However, he was a man of integrity and principles, was fair to Jim, and didn't look over his shoulder or unnecessarily bust his chops. Also, dealing with Mr. Dunn was infinitely better than being shackled with the senior partner, Douglas White, who essentially was Pol Pot with less personality and more anger.

White had once asked Jim to fire an associate stricken with cancer. "The guy's not pulling his weight. I don't care if he's sick, send him some flowers." Jim's interactions with "Old Man" White were very infrequent. For the last few years White had been pursuing goals loftier than the drudgery of his legal practice, such as debating which private golf course was the most challenging and appropriately restrictive, deciding which new legal secretary or associate would be his next guest at his condo in Point Pleasant and his never-ending quest to discover the perfect martini.

Chapter 5

Joe Devlin knew that Brenner wasn't much for chitchat. Today was no different. He'd asked several his best detectives to attend this meeting at his precinct, the 115. Harry raised his right hand to indicate that the room should come to attention and that he was ready to address them.

Once there was silence, Harry began, "As you all know, another body was discovered last night. This was the tenth one found in the last ten months within this precinct. At this point, we don't know what we're dealing with, maybe a serial killer, maybe not, which is the reason that I called you all here today. Our plan is to begin our investigation with the formation of a Task Force that will include each of you. This room will serve as the Command Center. I'll oversee this operation, with Detective Devlin supervising the Task Force and reporting directly to me. Every piece of information and correspondence will be shared with him. He will apprise me on our progress. I will share that information with the commissioner's office. I'll handle all press related matters. As we're all aware, the press has been on us about the possibility of a serial killer stalking Queens County, and if asked, you have no comment."

Brenner was in his mid-fifties. He was tall with salt and pepper hair, a strong jaw and a broad nose that had been broken once or twice. The Chief of Detectives wore a dark two-pieced suit, white shirt and navy blue and yellow striped tie. His deep-set chestnut eyes scanned the room. He took a few paces to his right and folded his arms over his chest.

"We're investigating homicides as we always do, and that's all that needs to be known. The public is already whispering about serial killers and nicknames and victim totals, and we can't have it. Make no mistake about it, gentlemen, we're up against it. But we'll smoke this person out and nail him to the wall. The public must know that they can walk the streets of their neighborhoods without fear in Queens County and throughout New York City."

As the liaison between the detectives and Brenner, Joe listened intently. He knew that this opportunity could make your career, or break it.

Brenner paused for a second to allow his words to sink in. Then, he continued. "As this is an extremely time-consuming and arduous task, we've cancelled vacations and days off for the foreseeable future to allow for you to concentrate all of your energy in finding this killer. The detectives not assigned to this Task Force will pick up the slack regarding your homicide cases. Some newly retired detectives are returning to the squad room to pitch in. I've been told that we can count on personnel and resource cooperation from the other boroughs of the city. We must all be on board, and this must be a cooperative effort. No pissing matches over boundary lines and who gets credit for what. Any issues should be brought to my attention immediately."

Joe noticed the detectives exchanging looks between each other. They were wearing nervous expressions on their faces. Some fidgeted with their watch or ring. Joe hadn't been a part of an investigation of this sort before and assumed the others hadn't either.

He watched as Brenner adjusted his tie, took a sip of water and said, "We'll begin with a briefing session tomorrow morning at 9:00 a.m. sharp. Spend the rest of the day reviewing the files and be prepared to work virtually non-stop until this criminal is in custody. The people and the NYPD brass have been heard from. Make it happen."

Brenner thanked the detectives for their time and dedication and hastily left the room, presumably to meet with the commissioner. Joe slumped down in his chair as the other detectives filed out, whispering about this task they'd just inherited. In the world of a homicide detective, you get accustomed to murders and dead bodies. There's always respect for the dead and anger toward the perpetrator, but murder is part and parcel of the vocation.

Joe thought about how some cases were different. Anything involving children snapped a cop out of his indifference. The thought of a serial killer made everyone's pants wet. Joe replayed Brenner's words repeatedly in his mind. Brenner was a top dog in the department who could write his own ticket if they pulled this off, as could Joe. But failure was a one-way ticket to checking parking meters in Peck, Idaho. Joe walked back to his desk, stared out the window for a few seconds and then sat down. He would knock off a little early tonight to beat the traffic back to Long Island, especially since he didn't know how much sleep he would get or how often he would see his wife once the Task Force began their tour tomorrow morning. Joe had one more item on his agenda before he went home. He picked up his cell phone.

"Hey, Joey, how's it going?" Al asked.

"Actually, not so great."

"What's wrong, what's troubling you?"

"Remember about five months ago, that thing we talked about after they found the body down by the river?"

"Of course. I may be retired but my mind still functions. I expected to hear from you today after I read the article in the paper. So, what do they think, serial killer?"

"Yeah, that's the scoop. They're forming a Task Force made of the top people in the NYPD to hunt down suspects. I'm supervising the operation and reporting to Brenner."

"They couldn't have picked a better man for the job," Al said. "But between me, you and the lamppost I wouldn't want this hot potato dropped in my lap. One of the newspapers hinted, well kinda suggested, that the killer could be a cop."

"I saw that, too, but Brenner never mentioned it. Today was more of an overview. They'll be a briefing tomorrow. Maybe he'll discuss that. And I hear what you're saying, but what can I do? You know how it is."

"Believe me, I know. For 28 years I put up with their crap. But this is different. If you don't deliver your pension will get as much mileage as the Edsel!"

"You always were a sweet talker, Al."

"Listen, the other side of the coin is that they know you're good, that you're a smart cop, and that means something. You have to get this nut off the street."

"Gotcha. I have no choice. My participation wasn't presented as an option. It's just a different type of investigation and I must get my head wrapped around it."

"I feel for you, kid, especially with what you and Patty went through. But even years ago I knew that you had it. Go with God."

"Thanks for your help."

"I didn't do anything, Joey, just listen."

"That's good enough. Be well, Al. Talk to you soon."

"I'm here if you need me. Anytime. Just call me. Oh, and Joey, watch your back."

"I always do, it's a hell of a lot better than my front."

Chapter 6

Jim exited the Long Island Railroad platform, walked down a flight of stairs and headed toward his vehicle. The end of another long Monday. Although he now had his Mercedes SUV for nine months, he still wasn't used to driving a fancy model. When he was a child, his parents had owned Dodge Darts and Plymouth Dusters. Good old-fashioned well-built American cars. But for his 45th birthday he decided to treat himself. He never took it for granted that he had more in the bank than most, nor did he have extravagant or ostentatious tastes. However, after what he had been through, he figured he deserved a "guilty pleasure."

A picture of his brother David entered his mind. With his sharp brown eyes, short straight brown hair and round face, the younger Bradley resembled his brother. His calloused hands from years on construction sites differed from Jim's smooth hands, which caressed a briefcase each day. David was so full of love for his family, especially his wife of six years, Michelle. She was a nurse and volunteered at several animal shelters. The two were never blessed with children, but travelled a lot, loved music, especially classic rock, and enjoyed sports. Jim had never encountered a more faithful, honest or trustworthy person than his brother. He could see them as kids running carelessly through the house, in their yard and on the ball field. Jim's lips pursed and his eyes moistened. He gripped the steering wheel, then wiped his eyes and took a deep breath.

At home Jim dropped his briefcase on the floor, placed his keys on the table to the left of the front door, and kissed Anakin. He went upstairs to change out of his suit and tie and into his walking clothes. He checked his three telephone messages. One was from his mom, "calling to see how my son is doing," the second was from a lady who wanted the homeowner to get in on the ground floor of the latest weight loss craze and the third was his dad, "calling to see how my son is doing." Jim assumed that it was a slow day down at his parents' condo in Tampa. He also knew that they worried about him, and held on very tightly since losing their other child.

Once downstairs he prepared a light dinner. He wasn't in the mood to cook, so he made himself a grilled cheese sandwich and paired it with some chips. Jim was tired of dinner for one, but at this point in his life he ate alone a lot. Anakin, having finished his meal, was now catching a quick snooze under the table near Jim's feet. He took advantage of the quiet to finally read the newspaper.

Both Raymond at *Coffee to go* and his boss had discussed current events with him, but this was the first opportunity he had to read the article in its entirety. He always read the paper in the correct fashion, beginning with the back and the sports section. After the information was adequately reviewed and digested, he turned the paper over to see the headline boldly staring up at him, *Body Found In Queens, Serial Killer Feared.* He read that the police source, commenting anonymously, had told the reporter that at present there were no legitimate leads. This source also stressed that the NYPD was doing everything in its power to find the culprits and bring them to justice, adding that a mass murderer was only one possibility and that all avenues were being explored. Jim wondered what the definition of "doing everything in its power" was to the NYPD, but nevertheless assumed that they had a plan of attack. He also knew that their plans were not always successful.

Jim scanned the article. It speculated that a member of the police could be the perpetrator. Many theories were presented, but Jim badly wanted to dismiss them because this thought was alarming. Still, he had experienced problems with law enforcement before. But cold-blooded multiple homicides. He pushed this possibility from his mind.

Again, Jim thought about how Dr. Lawrence had told him several times that there's no guarantee of safety in the world. Sometimes you had to take risks in order to live. This thought helped Jim: and he rarely worried about harm befalling him.

He finished the article, thumbed through the rest of the paper and finished his dinner. He grabbed Anakin's leash, latched it onto the collar surrounding his massive head, and made his way outside.

He walked down the driveway and made a left onto his street, Forest Avenue. Jim had a good pace going as he approached Thomas Jefferson Elementary School. Since he hadn't grown up in this town, Jim hadn't attended Jefferson, but the sight of the building, the ballfields and the grounds made him recall his carefree childhood days when he and his brother competed in the classroom and in the yard at their school. He remembered the moments when the two of them, only one year apart in age, talked about becoming professional baseball players.

"Breathe," he could hear his therapist say in his head. "As these thoughts approach, concentrate on your breathing, make that your focus." Jim thought about how he and his brother considered the days ahead when they would have children of their own. The cousins would grow up together and be regaled with stories about the path to pro baseball that began at Hamilton. Jim forced a smile as he picked up his pace, walking across the fields until he reached the end of school property and continued onto Pine Avenue.

As he approached the one-mile mark, Jim realized that he was in one of his frequent moods wherein he reviewed his life and took stock of himself. Over the last few years, he had become quite nostalgic, longing for his younger days of less stress and more fun. Lately Jim had been experiencing a regretful attitude. He was stagnating at work, hadn't had a meaningful relationship with a woman since his brother was killed, and felt as if he was running in place. Pleasure was a very distant cousin, except for his interaction with Anakin. This *woe is me* and *is this all there is* left him with a guilty and almost embarrassed after-taste, but he couldn't help what he felt.

And his unhappiness was getting worse.

Jim was three miles in. Anakin was stride for stride with him. The only problem was that his light meal had left him hungry. He rarely ate after 8:00 p.m., but tonight he'd make an exception. He detoured slightly so that he could enjoy the food and the ambiance of the Leaning Tower of Pizza, the best pizza place in the area. Jim strolled in and saw the owner, his buddy Vincenzo behind the counter.

Vincenzo said, "Whoa, look what the cat dragged in." His usual greeting for Jim. "I thought you health nuts only ate pizza on the weekend."

Vincenzo was right. Jim rarely came in during the week.

"How's my beautiful boy doing today?" asked Vincenzo as he scratched Anakin's back.

"I'm doing well," Jim said.

The friends shared a laugh. With a sparse crowd at this hour on a Monday night, Vincenzo allowed Anakin to stay inside at the entrance.

"I'll have two slices and a bottle of water to go please, Vin."

"You got it." Vincenzo wrapped up Jim's order. He always put a well-cooked meatball without sauce in the bag as well, a little treat for Anakin. "Have a good night, Jim."

"You too."

With his bag in one hand and Anakin's leash in the other, Jim pushed open the door with his foot. A voice called him as he was exiting.

"Hello, Counselor."

It was Jim's neighbor, Joe Devlin. They lived two houses apart, separated by the O'Connor house. Devlin had moved into the neighborhood about a year ago. He and Bradley hadn't interacted very often, just enough to exchange pleasantries.

When they moved onto the block, Jim had brought over food from the Leaning Tower to welcome them to the neighborhood. Joe's wife had been very friendly and appreciative, inviting him in for coffee and cake, but Joe was a little stand-offish. His demeanor began to change as they enjoyed the refreshments and got to know each other, exchanging stories about life as a cop and an attorney.

Joe had presented a rough and gruff exterior when he'd answered the door that day about a year ago, but since that night their few interactions had been friendly. However, their conversations were devoid of personal revelations, with Joe providing no information, nor asking Jim to provide any.

"Hello, Detective. How are you?"

"Fine, thanks. Long day. Patty told me she was going to bed early tonight, so I stopped in on my way home. I saw you and your buddy just as you were leaving."

"Yes, we're both on our way home to eat. I hate to say this Joe, but you look beat. Is everything okay?"

"I'm sure you've seen the stories in the news by now about the possibility of a serial killer being responsible for a string of deaths in Queens?"

"Sure I have. Are you in on the investigation?"

"Yeah, I'm the lead investigator on a Task Force. We've got the Feds involved too."

"So, it's true then, no longer speculation? The murders were the result of a serial killer?"

"Let's just say that I will invoke cop-attorney privilege, or neighbor-attorney privilege, and tell you yes, we are operating under that assumption. I'm sure it will be all over the place by morning."

"I really feel for the victims, Joe, and their families. The pain and agony is overwhelming. I don't know if you know, but my brother David was violently killed six years ago.

Since then…well…I've never gotten over it. Please let me know if I can help in any way. Not just as an attorney, but as a neighbor and hopefully a friend." Jim's eyes gazed the pavement.

"I'm very sorry for your loss. I wasn't aware. Patty and I can understand your pain. It's a terrible coincidence…our son Thomas was killed eight years ago. We aren't whole, either. Actually, we're in pieces."

"Oh, Joe, I'm so sorry. I didn't know. I hope what I said didn't dig up those memories."

"No, they were never buried. You've been there. It's a nightmare you never wake up from. Anyway, sorry again."

The two men began to walk home, with Anakin between them. They arrived at the detective's place first.

"Joe, please, feel free to call on me to bounce ideas off, brainstorm, whatever. I would love to be useful in any way I can. It might even bring a little peace."

"For both of us, hopefully. Goodnight, Jim."

"Goodnight, and good luck."

Once in the house, Jim devoured the slices, gulped down the water and gave his pal the special present from Vincenzo. He mulled over Joe's revelation. Jim found it incredibly ironic that both he and Joe lost a loved one to violent crime.

Anakin chewed the meatball with a look of satisfaction that made Jim smile. He loved seeing his best friend feeling content. As he made his way up to his bedroom for a hot shower, Anakin followed one step behind.

After washing the day off his body, Jim relaxed in bed with his 120-pound pooch curled up at his feet. Anakin looked up at Jim with gleaming eyes, as if he could read his mind. Anakin possessed deep and soulful almond shaped eyes, had a beautiful black coat with mahogany markings above each eye and muzzle. He was lazy also. Jim once told his mom that Anakin began his day by going back to bed. On cue, the Rottweiler laid back in his sleeping position as Jim flipped on the television.

A quick roundup of the day's sporting events first, and then onto the news. He had turned a local channel on just in time to hear about the possible serial killer stalking the streets of Queens. He listened with one ear only as much of the information was the same as what had appeared in the newspaper, including the chance that the police were looking for one of their own. Jim began to drift off, and the last thing he heard was a police department official taking about the creation of a Task Force to investigate the homicides.

When his alarm blared at 6:00 a.m. Jim threw off his blanket. Downstairs he poured himself first one, then a second cup of coffee. Jim had slept a little better and a little longer than the night before, so he had more pep in his step on this Tuesday morning. He anticipated further conversations with Raymond from *Coffee to go* and his boss about the story rattling the public.

He eased into his seat on the train and began to thumb through the newspaper. The first few pages were all a repeat. Jim perused the articles with mild irritation. At this point, the same facts and worries were being reiterated repeatedly. What was the good of scaring the public if there were no breaks in the case? Later in the day, he'd check the Internet to see if anything had changed.

After nodding off for a few moments, he awoke as the train pulled into Penn Station. As he exited the train, he mentally mapped out his schedule. Jim hoped he would arrive back from the courthouse after "Old Man" White had already left for the day, which often was before lunch.

Jim wondered if Douglas White was affected at all by the killings, if he felt for the families of the victims, as William Dunn did. Perhaps he was too rich, powerful, and aloof to care about people in Queens. Maybe White's money and status made him feel separated from the daily drudgery of murder. This thought did not sit well with Jim. While White was not a strong leader, he had been an accomplished litigator in his day. But the idea that the senior partner probably lacked empathy for people dying in Queens made Jim feel nothing but contempt for him.

Chapter 7

Joe Devlin had just merged onto the Long Island Expressway early Tuesday morning and was mulling over the phone call he'd received the previous evening from Brenner. Joe had expected to have a one-on-one meeting with him, but it never came to fruition. However, once home, Joe had answered the phone and found Harry at the other end of the line. Devlin was instructed to report to One Police Plaza in Manhattan prior to going to his precinct in Queens. He'd meet there with Brenner, Lieutenant Moss and some uniformed officers for a briefing with Commissioner Ted Fields. Joe had a notion that more players would be part of this game, but Brenner wasn't divulging or volunteering any more names over the phone.

During their conversation, Brenner explained that Joe would be responsible for relaying the high points of the meeting to the other Task Force members, which now included some uniformed officers. "The brass wants some experienced foot and motor vehicle patrol cops to lend support and manpower to the Task Force's investigation."

Joe translated that message as: pressure had been put on the commissioner from any combination of media outlets and interest groups, and he'd like some personnel on the street whose interrogation techniques might not conform to what the ACLU deemed appropriate.

Brenner said, "Commissioner Fields wasn't pleased that the nightly news had run with the serial killer angle. It inflames and frightens the public."

Joe knew that the big wigs weren't exactly choked up about the discussion of the formation of a police manhunt.

Brenner, like his compadres, played it close to the vest and conservative, only sharing information with John Q. Public as they saw fit.

"As you know, Joe, with social media, it's next to impossible to keep these details in-house. I dread the flood of phony and false leads and tips, and inquiries regarding possible rewards. It mucks up the works and takes time away from legitimate leads."

Joe hung up with Brenner after an hour discussion. As he got ready for bed, his head was spinning, his stomach churning. He wanted to call his old pal Al, but there was plenty of time over the next few weeks and possibly months for that. Al turned in early.

Joe's wife Patricia had asked if there was anything he would like to talk about that evening. Joe was an old school kind of a guy, a Gary Cooper strong silent type. He rarely discussed his work-related problems with Patty. General talk he was fine with, but he shied away from specific details. As he didn't wish to further burden her, Joe mentioned that he was a little run down and just needed some rest. His wife wondered aloud if maybe Joe could relax this weekend. He mumbled too low for Patricia to hear, "Only if they catch this bastard in the next three days." Unfortunately, the brass owned him until the case was closed.

The subject of the Task Force never came up, and Joe never let on to her that tomorrow he would be engaged in anything but routine police work, if there were such a thing. At a later date, he might have no choice but to divulge that information, but why make her worry needlessly until he had a firmer grasp of what he was dealing with? His hope was that the next day some questions would be answered. But his experience and sixth sense told him that it would only bring more questions.

While stuck in traffic, Joe's focus changed from a recounting of last night's events to the road ahead of him. He was used to his commute each morning from his Nassau

County home to his precinct in Queens, but today he left his house earlier in preparation for congestion on his way into Manhattan. Joe could have taken the LIRR as his neighbors who commuted into the Big Apple did, but he didn't care for trains and preferred to have his car with him in case of an emergency.

He vacillated between pride and anger regarding his inclusion in this investigation. Of course, he was flattered to be asked not only to participate, but to be one of the leaders. An essential cog who would serve as an intermediary between the decision makers and those who the decisions affected. But he figured that if this was a plum assignment, it would have been given to one of the up-and-coming puppets who spent their days dreaming of 40-foot Sea Ray yachts. However, he did have the respect of his superiors. Joe was thought of as a tough, no-nonsense guy who had closed some major cases and was able to know when a little butt-kicking was called for and when a little humanity was required. But he was only involved in one serial killer investigation, and that was on a peripheral level many years ago. Now he was the point man in the foremost investigation in New York City.

Joe was unable to get into the mind of a serial killer. The drug pushers and violent criminals weren't difficult to figure out, and his beat-cop experience had given him a razor-sharp eye and a good ear. Al constantly reminded him, "Pay close attention to the spoken. Pay even more attention to the unspoken. Always keep your eyes and ears open."

Joe realized that this investigation would open the door to a new world. His studying had educated him to the fact that a serial killer was an entirely different animal than the kind he interacted with daily. He had a cerebral nature which, when coupled with a visceral disposition, made for the most dangerous slayer. Joe knew that if there was no motive and they were searching for a psychopath or sociopath without an agenda or pattern, they were in deep trouble.

Joe it a cigarette and changed the radio station. He'd slept poorly in anticipation of the meeting this morning and the long, arduous days ahead. He flipped from one news radio station to the other, attempting to absorb as much information as possible and trying to ascertain if any news outlet had more knowledge of the goings on than he did.

He put on some music for a while before changing to an all-sports radio station. Joe figured that if he was going to get aggravated, he might as well listen to his fellow New York Jets fans discuss and argue with the host about Sunday's loss. He remembered hearing the Jets coach lamenting certain plays at his press conference and explaining that they were a play or two away from winning the game. At this moment, Joe wondered if he and his team were a play or two away from winning *their* game. He also wondered if the Jets coach would want to trade troubles or salaries with him, or if it was too late to become the shortstop for the New York Mets.

As Joe navigated his way over the Williamsburg Bridge, he allowed some anger to creep into his thoughts. "Why the hell is this killer on the loose now?" he asked in a curt tone. He didn't need this crap, especially after what he and his wife had been through.

Both Joe and Patty had suffered from anger, rage and chronic grief. The grief turned to depression, and they had both battled suicidal thoughts. They were left with emptiness and numbness. Joe's ability to work became impaired, causing him to take a leave of absence from the job. Patty quit her job and pulled away from social interactions. Joe desperately encouraged her to leave the house.

He recalled a conversation they'd had about a year after Thomas' murder, a dialogue that had been re-visited on several occasions. "You've got to get outside a little Patty, engage in some activities that you used to like. Go back to playing tennis or volunteering. Maybe get a part-time job. I'm worried about you."

"My heart's just not in it, Joe. I'm not ready. I need some

more time. Please understand.”

Joe understood all too well, but he knew if Patty didn’t soon find a reason to leave the house soon, she might never do so. And her health was deteriorating along with her will. Her persistent stomach pains, headaches and hypertension forced her to make doctor appointments and emergency room visits.

The detective had first balked at therapy, but Patty felt it might be beneficial. They first went as a couple. When the analysis felt ineffective, they attempted counseling individually. The continual reliving of that awful day proved too weighty for them, and they ultimately stopped going.

Finally, Joe arrived at his destination, located in downtown Manhattan near City Hall. Joe pulled into a spot in the parking garage beneath the building. He lit another Marlboro, took a sip of coffee and turned the radio first down, then off completely. He quickly reviewed the high notes and bullet points from yesterday’s meeting with Brenner. Shortly, he would be in the room with his boss and some heavy hitters. These were the types of men who could turn your pension papers into either the lining of a birdcage or an accessory in the men’s restroom.

Joe knew the streets; he knew criminals and their motives. He knew the criminal spectrum from the organized crime boss to the low-level dealer. Joe figured that once he got past all this administrative nonsense and got down to real police work, he could sink his teeth into tracking down this killer. He felt he had a good chance to succeed, but he also knew that success was expected and not negotiable. As his old partner used to tell him, “Joseph my boy, a child tries, a man accomplishes.”

Chapter 8

Joe didn't want to be at the meeting early and he definitely didn't want to be late. Truth be told he didn't want to be there at all. As he exited his car, he took one last drag on his smoke and then tossed it on the pavement of the parking garage, crushing it out with his foot.

He arrived at 8:55 sharp. Similar to former Giants coach Tom Coughlin, Brenner felt that if you arrived right on time, you were late. Brenner greeted Joe at the door with a handshake and a lukewarm "good morning." As Joe made his way around the room saying his hellos, he realized that an all-star lineup was assembled. Lieutenant George Moss, Borough Detective Amanda Gordon and a number of uniformed cops.

In addition, Brenner had told him the previous evening that Captain Frank Sterling would be present. Sterling was Joe's Captain and had made his bones years ago in Manhattan South. He'd bolstered his reputation as a tough guy by almost beating a longshoreman to death in the parking lot of Caravallo's restaurant in Brooklyn after the longshoreman had disrespected the first Mrs. Sterling (The second Mrs. Sterling was about 15 years his junior and was probably in grade school on that fateful night).

One of the players in the room not divulged to Devlin beforehand was a very distinguished looking gentleman who Joe had never seen before. Said gentleman was thin and looked in his mid-forties with wire-rimmed glasses and short, wavy black hair. His dark blue suit was complimented with a light blue shirt and cherry-red tie. He was positioned immediately to Commissioner Fields' left. Following the appropriate exchange of pleasantries, everyone took their seats to await their marching orders.

Commissioner Fields began with a recapitulation of Devlin's prior meeting with Brenner. Essentially, Devlin would run the Task Force and would function as a liaison between the brass and the uniformed and plain clothed personnel who would be on the street investigating and chasing leads.

"Lieutenant Moss will serve to facilitate communication between Joe Devlin and Harry Brenner," said the commissioner. "And Brenner will funnel information to and from 1PP, as well as politicians and the media. The Task Force will work out of the 115. This will be a collaborative and cooperative effort. Everyone will have the same goal, the same purpose and will be on the same team."

Joe knew the commissioner was appealing to their desire for justice, as well as their retirement and their overtime. Joe glanced around the room, noting that Fields had gotten their attention. Most cops, he realized, would walk barefoot over hot coals to protect their pension and OT.

As the commissioner continued, Joe thought about the assailant's choice of weapon. The semi-automatic pistol m1911 contained a magazine filled with rounds usually carried in the gun's handle. After every shot the force of the recoil moved the top part (the slide) back, throwing out the used case and picking up a new round on its way back. Joe recalled that they had found a used case at each crime scene, but never found a print on any of them. This was a fastidious fellow, thought Devlin, cleaning off each case prior to loading his weapon. Semi-autos could be quite thin, very light and convenient for everyday concealed carry. A silencer, or suppressor, also worked best on semi autos. However, unlike revolvers, they were harder to handle for a novice shooter. *Did this mean our killer was an experienced shooter, maybe former military or law enforcement?* So far, this question hadn't been broached by Brenner or Fields.

Fields said, "The NYPD has asked the FBI for assistance in certain areas of expertise, such as psychological profiling and advanced forensic techniques. The FBI would also have resources beyond the NYPD, and their involvement would increase the number of people working on the case and gathering evidence. This will be an NYPD investigation, and the FBI is here to support us. Every courtesy was to be extended to the Feds."

The man to the Commissioner's left had not yet been identified. But Joe didn't need to be a returning "Jeopardy" champion to realize that the man who nobody in the room (except Fields) was acquainted with was an FBI guy. Right on cue, Ted segued into the introduction of FBI Criminal Profiler Russell Hollander. The Commissioner quickly corrected himself, explaining that technically there's no such thing at the Bureau as profilers – they're called analysts. Fields shook hands with Hollander, the Task Force members said their "hellos" and "good mornings," and Ted turned the floor over to him.

Before Hollander began to address his new co-workers, Devlin took a moment to consider this Fed. Joe assumed he had flown up from Washington D.C. yesterday and was briefed by Sterling and Fields prior to a five-star lobster and steak dinner (at the expense of the New York City taxpayers). The night was probably capped off with a reservation at an executive suite in a swanky Manhattan hotel overlooking Central Park, where Hollander would be met with champagne, strawberries, chocolates and a nice surprise waiting for him in his king size bed (the price for these perks would also be picked by the good citizens of NYC). But Joe digressed. His thoughts just seemed to wander away from him, especially lately. He re-gained his focus and studied Hollander as he began to address his audience.

"Good morning. Commissioner Fields reached out to me because of my vast experience in this area. My job is to get into the mind of the killer given certain clues, and to attempt to explain and predict serial criminal activity. Our team has spent many hours researching the psychopathic mind, and we are skilled in analyzing physical evidence like fingerprints and footprints."

Hollander pushed back his thinning hair where it had drifted down to his forehead. "Generally, a serial killer keeps going until one of four things happens: he is caught, he dies, he kills himself or he burns out. A serial killer presents a different threat than a street criminal, and thus must be investigated using different techniques.

"Although their motivation may vary, certain procedural similarities are common among them, and enable us to construct a very general profile. Please keep in mind that some of the characteristics I'll discuss are generalities, and many serial killers may fall outside the bell curve. However, it's a good place to start."

Joe looked around the room and saw his colleagues staring intently at Hollander, their bodies upright, their brows raised, seemingly hanging on every word. Joe surmised that there had to be heat on the commissioner for him to get the o.k. to recruit one of Washington's stars to provide assistance and support in an NYPD investigation.   Hollander inspected his fingernails and pressed on. "Serial killers tend to be mostly white males, between 20 and 45 years of age. They frequently suffer from low self-esteem and tend to be introverted and friendless. They are often loners who will depart the social norms and tend to inhabit an imaginary world. Their fantasies begin small and merely imagining scenarios can gratify them. But for those who develop into killers, at some point these imaginary scenarios start to become insufficient.

"This is a big step, even for a highly aberrant mind. Many of the serial killers I have interrogated admitted that they relived their actions over and over in their mind, thus receiving again that gratification obtained during the actual murder. They also told me that, by doing so, they were setting the stage for their progression."

Hollander adjusted his sapphire cuffliks. "Let's spend some time discussing *our guy*. What do we know about the ten victims? Well, for starters, there have been six men and four women. Each D.O.A was either a sex worker, homeless or a drug user. Their bodies were found in predominantly poor and isolated areas within Queens County."

"These people make easier targets, as they're willing to go with the perpetrator or at least engage in conversation with the lure of money or drugs. In addition, these individuals can often drop out of site without the bells and whistles that would go off if a working mother, suburban housewife or accountant went missing. Also, we all know from our experience, crimes in low-income areas don't generate the buzz that those in richer areas creates. These factors may provide an explanation as to why it took until the tenth body was found to determine that we were dealing with this type of criminal."

Joe, who had been hanging on every word, pressed his lips firmly together. He eschewed eye contact with both Moss and Brenner. Joe had told both, when the fifth victim was found at an abandoned warehouse, that these were not random unconnected acts. But they instructed Joe and the other detectives to proceed as if it were a usual murder. Joe had the feeling in his gut after the fourth victim was found that something was amiss. He shared his initial hunch only with his ex-partner.

The two had been enjoying a few beers on a Saturday afternoon when Joe raised the subject with Al. "I've got a strange feeling in my bones," Joe said. "This one just keeps gnawing at me. I've spent the last several weeks going over it again and again. I know it's the same guy. Maybe it's just instinct, or maybe I keep hearing my old partner and his wise teachings."

Silvani had a wry smile and took a meaningful swig of his Heineken. "We've both been through this hell before. You know how it goes Joey. Like the guy said in *Jaws*, you yell barracuda, and everyone says 'what, huh?' But you yell shark and you've got hysteria on your hands. It's the same thing with these psychos. You yell murderer and you get some attention, but you yell serial killer, and the city hits the panic button. It's a whole different mindset. They'll operate under the assumption that it's not the same guy for as long as they can, until their hand is forced."

Joe had to agree. Al always provided keen and provoking insights. Joe missed working with his old partner very much, especially for the stories, anecdotes and life-lessons. As he took a healthy bite out of his burger, Joe told Al, "I'll keep you informed."

Al nodded, wiped his mouth, and ordered a second Heineken.

Joe turned his attention back to Russell Hollander's briefing. "As I previously stated, a remote or secluded area, a place where he can discard the victim's body quickly without the likelihood of being seen, is the type of locale which best suits the killer's needs. However, in our current case, it seems that the whole violent episode occurs at one location. The victims weren't transported, but rather were murdered and left right there."

Hollander took a sip from his mug. "Besides this fact, what else do we know? Well, our guy hasn't left a trace of physical evidence and no DNA. The victims were killed with a single shot, suggesting our perp may have a military or law enforcement background. His weapon is a semi-automatic pistol m1911."

Joe's eyes widened when Hollander conjectured about the possible involvement of an individual within the criminal justice system. Not wanting to make eye contact with Fields or Brenner, he kept his stare on their FBI guest.

"Let me take a step back," said Hollander. "The profile I'm describing is only that, a profile. People who kill strangers all have their own reasons for their actions. The scariest thought is that our guy could be seemingly normal, someone you went to high school with. Many serial killers aren't reclusive social misfits who live alone, despite depictions of them in the news and in entertainment. Often, they don't appear to be strange or stand out from the public in any meaningful way. Those who blend in are typically also employed, have families and homes and outwardly appear to be non-threatening, normal members of society."

With that Hollander ended his briefing, which Joe found not very brief. Yet he knew it was essential. Everyone said their good-byes and wished each other good luck, which they desperately needed.

Joe sat at a desk and watched as the others filed out of the room. He closed his eyes to let Hollander's words register. He also pondered the impact being the lead investigator on this case would have on Patty. The 75–80-hour weeks would be tough on her. She always had forgiven the long hours, but over the last few years she'd struggled being alone. Joe recognized that she was best thing that had ever happened to him. The quicker he wrapped up this case, the quicker he could return to his usual detective work and to normalcy. Although Joe knew things could never be normal again for Patty and him.

Chapter 9

James Bradley awoke to a blaring alarm and Anakin cuddled up next to him. In happier days he had awoken with a sexy blonde or curvy brunette. Jim was never a one-night stand type of guy. He had two serious relationships and had felt marriage was on the horizon in both cases. Neither one had worked out.

Ashley Sommers was an attorney at Wallace & Pruitt, in the same building as Jim's firm. She was the sexy blonde. They met at Raymond's *Coffee to Go* in the lobby and moved on to lunch and eventually to dinner. Each time the subject of matrimony was discussed, Ashley balked. "It's not the right time, Jim," or, "We're getting along so well, why should we risk marriage?"

After six years Jim realized that she didn't want to get married, or didn't want to marry him, so they broke up amicably. Ashley was now a partner at Wallace & Pruitt, and she sported a new name, Ashley Wallace.

Connie DeMarco was a buyer for Bloomingdale's. She was the curvy brunette. They were introduced at a party given by a mutual friend and hit it off immediately. Again, Jim heard wedding bells, but Connie must have heard a different tune. Also, her parents were not thrilled with the possibility of their grandkids bearing a last name ending with a consonant instead of a vowel. Their disapproval and her need to please them unconditionally ripped at the soul of their relationship, causing its termination.

Before David was killed, Jim wasn't content with his unmarried status. But since his brother's death, it had been very hard for him to maintain a relationship with a woman, even though he craved one. Sometimes he thought he was better suited to be single. Other times he longed for the love, companionship and support that marriage could provide. Since losing David, he's also lost the ability to sustain any closeness with others and the confidence that his judgment was clear.

However, Jim was not complaining about waking next to Anakin, as he required less energy than most of his ex-girlfriends and was easier on the wallet and the blood pressure.

He made his way downstairs, still with sleep in his eyes and running his hands through his hair, with Anakin at his heels. Jim always took care of his dog first, laying out his food and water, and then letting him outside the back sliding glass door to roam the yard for a while.

Today would be a long day, as most were. Something light for breakfast, a toasted bagel with cream cheese and coffee, very sweet. As Jim sat down, he slid his newspaper out of the clear plastic wrap and began to peruse the previous day's headlines. Jim realized that most of his younger co-workers and colleagues, and even many of his contemporaries, got their news via phone, tablet or laptop. Some of the "20 somethings" in the office regarded a newspaper as having gone the way of the dinosaur or akin to stone tablets. But he was old-fashioned.

Jim reviewed the articles and editorials regarding the possibility of a serial killer terrorizing the Big Apple. One of the articles stated that the bodies of up to ten victims had been found in New York City, and more specifically Queens, over the last year. "Are they connected?" wondered Jim's newspaper, the *Long Island News*. According to the story, the NYPD had formed a Task Force and now the FBI had joined the hunt.

Jim was proud of his neighbor, Detective Joe Devlin, for his assignment as leader of the Task Force. He prayed for Joe's success in ending the city's misery. Jim would reach out again to him, offering support and help in any way possible. He hated the idea that families would have to go through the horror his did.

Some articles cited anonymous police sources as the genesis of their information. The police force had more people gossiping than TMZ. But this was no surprise to him, based on his prior dealings with law enforcement.

Since David's death, he had become pessimistic, irritable, and bitter. The incompetence of the police in their botched investigation and the ineptness of the District Attorney's office in the prosecution of the killer served as a springboard for his simmering rage. This was a metamorphosis even Gregor Samsa would be shocked by. But he was glad Joe was handling this case. Jim trusted his neighbor.

Jim didn't wish to begin what would already be an arduous and stressful day in this toxic mind frame. As Anakin peered in at Jim through the sliding glass back door, his expression informed his master that he had taken care of his business, gotten his requisite exercise and was ready to come inside for his post-breakfast nap. It also reminded Jim that he'd spent too much time dwelling on the past this morning (and in general), and that he now had to hurry up to catch his train. The sliding glass door was opened and Jim's thoughts now turned to getting ready for work and his lunch meeting with the esteemed William Dunn.

Jim scurried past the legal secretaries and went into his office, which was right next to the one occupied by Dunn. His boss' office was significantly larger and better decorated, but Jim didn't want to focus on that fact.

Around 11:00 a.m., Dunn poked his head into Jim's office to remind him of their 1:00 p.m. lunch appointment. His boss was an incredible creature of habit, reminding Jim each time of their lunch engagement, even though the two had lunch every Wednesday at 1:00 p.m., except for court appearances and vacations.

They dined at the Mortimer Club on 52nd Street going on about five years now. Despite the snooty name, the food was good, the portions substantial and the ambiance relaxed (and the firm or Bill picked up the tab so why should Jim complain?) Jim assured Dunn that their "lunch date" was still on, and Dunn hurried off, presumably to check off this item on his to-do list. Jim shook his head and chuckled at Dunn's fastidious nature, but not in a derisive way. His boss was a dynamo, with the ability to keep many balls in the air at the same time while staying grounded. Jim was impressed and had to give him a lot of credit.

Jim sat behind his desk, pushed some papers around, then rubbed his weary eyes vigorously. He had some time before lunch to tackle work but would rather undergo root canal without anesthesia. He walked over to his window and stared down at midtown Manhattan.

Jim thought of one of his favorite movies, *The Third Man*, starring Orson Welles. Welles character, Harry Lime, looks down from his seat on a Ferris wheel and sees the people below as dots moving around. That's how they appeared to Jim from his 16th floor window. From this distance, Jim felt isolated from them and aloof. Although he wished the walkers no harm, he perceived them as insignificant and irrelevant. This struck him as ironic, since that was the same perception he had about himself.

Chapter 10

As Jim and Bill passed the *Coffee to Go* shop on their way to lunch, Ray got their attention, calling them over to get their thoughts on the explosive headline.

"What do you think, another Son of Sam?" Ray referenced David Berkowiz, the .44 caliber killer who had terrorized New York City in the summer of 1977.

"I only know what I've been reading in the papers," Dunn said. "Hard to say at this point."

"It is a little early to start speculating about who the guy is or his motive," Jim said. "On the other hand, if the news is accurate and ten bodies have been discovered, the cops better catch this maniac or you'll see a panic similar to the Son of Sam search."

William and Ray both nodded in agreement.

Ironically, all three men were pre-teens when David Berkowitz had been apprehended in 1977. However, they could recollect the conversations at the dinner table when their parents discussed him. Bradley was amazed at the things he could recall from his childhood. There was innocence and a hopefulness that existed when he was growing up, feelings that had long ago been washed away and swept out to sea.

When he was a boy, his parents told him that if he worked hard, if he behaved, he would be able to achieve his goals. No mention was ever made of what it would feel like when the train went off the tracks and derailed. His parents protected him from the harsh realities of life. Endless Wiffle ball games, school events and dates had been replaced with countless sleep-deprived nights and dinner for one in front of the television. Hope had been replaced by monotony, innocence by cynicism.

Jim recalled the day David brought Michelle home to announce their engagement. Jim had met her first when he'd spoken to her fourth-grade class at a career day. But she and David had fallen in love a few months later when he built a deck onto her parents' home. Unfortunately, they never had children, as Jim felt they would've made terrific parents. At least they'd found each other yet had so much more of life to experience together, which made David's murder even more horrible.

His mood became somber and melancholy and was brought back to the present by William Dunn, sitting across from him. Jim and Bill had been escorted to their usual table at the Mortimer club by the maître d, Walter Dempsey. Walt was a good-natured Irishman, with a quick wit, a light for your cigar and an extended hand, ready to be garnished with the green stuff (cash, not parsley). It was a typical Wednesday crowd. Jim saw virtually the same people here each Wednesday. Not many strolled into the Mortimer Club casually, especially since the menu in the window advertised prices as long as phone numbers. As a result, the Club had a consistent and familiar list of patrons.

The two attorneys accepted their menus from their waiter, Albert, who waited on these gents almost every week. The menu was a polite gesture. Both knew it by heart. Albert gave his usual spiel about the specials, which they half listened to and then nodded a thank you. William gave the menu a perusal and wasn't against ordering a different item each week. This played against his general personality, but Dunn said that when it came to food and women, there was nothing wrong with a little variety.

William ordered two glasses of wine (Jim assumed one was for him), removed his glasses, placed them in their holder and into his inside jacket pocket. Jim observed his swiftness in accomplishing this task, which meant that he had something on his mind.

When William's glasses removal was deliberate, Jim knew that meant their conversation would be on the light side: sports, musings about life, office gossip and other non-serious topics. But a quick glasses removal meant he had a more important bee in his bonnet. Bill Dunn was so easy to read that Jim would love to play poker with him. Jim was guessing that the subject was not law firm related, but rather the topic that was on the front page, leading news telecasts and being discussed in the office, as well as by their mutual friend Raymond at *Coffee to Go*.

"I didn't want to get into a long discussion with Ray at the coffee shop earlier. We were rushing to get here and with all those people hustling to lunch I felt the time wasn't appropriate for such a sensitive topic. I like Ray a lot, he's a very nice man. I hope he didn't feel put off. Do you think I was rude not to discuss his question longer?"

"Not at all," said Jim. "Like you said, Ray's a good guy and not the type to be overly sensitive. We've known each other for years, and he understands we were in a hurry. Also, Ray won't miss a chance to corner you again and ask you. So forget it. There'll be plenty of opportunities for discussion."

Jim had to allay his boss' anxiety over the possible slight so Dunn would be able to relax and enjoy his lunch. Along with being a model of efficiency, Dunn was a chronic worrier, especially when it came to dealing with others, particularly subordinates. Dunn treated everyone equally and didn't see the world as a caste system. He chafed at the idea that he made another feel inadequate or insignificant. If Jim couldn't put Dunn's mind at ease, they wouldn't be able to get past it. That would cause the butt-kissing they'd receive throughout the meal from the staff to not have its full effect.

Dunn sniffed then sipped his wine, and a smile came to his face as the stuffed mushrooms arrived. Jim could see in Bill's relaxed body language and calm expression that the burden of his guilt had been removed.

"So, what are your thoughts about the big headline today?"

"It's hard to know what to think," Jim answered. "It's so shocking."

"I heard some conflicting reports," said Dunn, "both on TV and in the papers questioning if these murders are the result of a serial killer or merely random acts of violence. There are a lot of crazy people in the world. This doesn't necessarily have to be the work of one individual." Dunn paused for a moment at that thought, as if he wasn't sure which of the two possibilities caused him greater concern.

Jim had been splitting his attention between his meal and listening to Dunn's theories. He was far more interested in the sizzling steak and succulent lobster, but he feigned interest in his boss' thoughts.

At the meal's conclusion, Albert came over to collect the dishes and wine glasses and to see if either man was interested in dessert or coffee. They complimented the meal and the wine but told Albert that they'd pass on dessert and coffee. He hustled away and said he would bring the check. Dunn picked up the tab every time. He had a generous expense account and these meals were a perk that the junior partners received from the more senior partners for their work efforts. Dunn had once told Jim that Old Man White never questioned his partners' expenses. "Why would he?" thought Jim. A man in White's powerful position couldn't be dragged away from his Vegas trips or Bahamas junkets to perform the menial task of reviewing expense reports.

As soon as Albert was out of sight, Jim began to address his boss' concerns.

"I wouldn't press the panic button just yet. But you never know how the public will react to this type of thing. Fear can spread and make people do odd things or make strange decisions. I don't want to give into fear at this point. We need to wait and see how and where it goes.

"To your point regarding one killer or many killers, my

neighbor is an NYPD detective who is now the lead investigator on a Task Force. He told me a few days ago that the purpose of its creation was to hunt down a serial killer. And I don't mind telling you the idea of this causes me anxiety. As you know, my brother was violently killed. In addition, when my parents read or hear the news they'll be very worried. Losing a child has obviously made them overly concerned about my safety and welfare. This has conjured up bad memories."

Albert brought over the check, accompanied by a few decadent pieces of chocolate on a silver tray. The men split the four pieces and William took care of the check. Jim used to ask for the bill, but William never allowed him to pay. This went on for some time but became tedious and Jim now just accepted his boss' largesse.

On their walk back to the firm, Bill stopped about twenty feet from the entrance and turned to face Jim. "I know what you and your family have been through with your brother, and I'd be genuinely sorry and embarrassed if I brought back terrible memories or if you felt that I was in any way apathetic on the subject of death."

Jim stared into the October sun. A slight fall breeze flapped the lapels of his suit jacket. His stare moved from the sun to Dunn's face. He considered his boss and his words very carefully. Dunn was not the usual type found in positions of influence at blue blood law firms. He was sensitive in a business that was often insensitive, caring in a never-ending sea of apathy and able to see his employees as individuals, rather than merely means to a profitable end.

"I never feel you're anything but respectful and considerate," assured Jim. "You were kind when I needed kindness and a good sounding board when I needed to vent. As you recall, it was very hard for me to function at work after my brother's death. I was dragging myself to the office, sleep deprived and unable to concentrate."

Jim held his hand out for Bill to shake, which he gladly

obliged. "If I didn't say it before, I apologize, but I'll say it now. Thank you, Bill, for being there for me during the hard times and the rough days after David was killed. It was greatly appreciated. No matter what happened at the firm, I always knew I had at least one true ally. I don't know why it took so long for me to say this to you, but I'm grateful."

Dunn was a cool man, a difficult man to throw off stride or catch by surprise, but he seemed to be overwhelmed by Jim's words. His face became flushed and his mouth fell open, but no words came out.

"Hope I didn't embarrass you," Jim said sheepishly. "I just needed to get that off my chest and I felt that now was the right time to do so."

Bill nodded. "No, not at all, and no apology is necessary. Your frankness is refreshing."

Jim flashed a smile. "Now that we have begun our Mutual Admiration Society, we probably should go inside and get back to work, before people think we headed to Vegas for a quickie wedding."

"Sure thing," agreed Bill, and the two men continued walking to their building, each with a busy Wednesday afternoon to look forward to.

Chapter 11

Det. Devlin awoke very early following a sleepless night of tossing and turning and *Gilligan's Island* reruns. Today would be the first day of his assignment as the lead investigator of the Joint Task Force and he was anxious to get started.

Following a nutritious breakfast of cigarettes and black coffee, Devlin retrieved his garbage cans from the curb and got into his car. He took a long drag on the Marlboro he'd lit immediately upon starting the engine, then rubbed his left temple with his thumb.

The Joint Task Force would work out of Joe's Queens precinct, where he felt comfortable. He knew he could expect a lot of company from the higher-ups at One Police Plaza, and possibly some politicians who wanted the public to believe they were rolling up their sleeves and pitching in. Day one was always the most difficult and tedious in any investigatory process. Most of the members of the Joint Task Force were present yesterday at the briefing conducted by FBI Agent Russell Hollander. However, last night Joe had been advised that a few more individuals had been added. These lucky few "volunteers" would need Joe to give them the *Reader's Digest* version of Hollander's tutorial, plus any supplemental tidbits that Joe needed to impart.

Joe had a phone conversation with Al Silvani last night just to bounce some ideas off him. He loved his former partner' s way of calling him "Joey." Everyone was "pal," "bud," "ace" or "cheech" to Al. If he thought you were a fool, you were a "stugotz." All of these nicknames were given further texture by a Brooklyn accent that Al could never shake. Joe always thought of him as a cross between a Jewish mother and an Italian father. Al would feed and coddle you, and he could give you a thorough tongue-lashing, depending on which approach he deemed most effective at the time. His fellow officers loved him and would take a bullet for him. They knew, as Joe did, that he always had their back.

During their phone conversation, Al stressed the importance of building relationships with both the members of the community and the Task Force. Of shedding territorial egos to further cooperation. "Remember Joey, you got Feds, captains, detectives, lieutenants and beat cops all on the same team. Not everyone may be pulling in the same direction. You gotta get everyone to buy into a single purpose, a single mission and goal."

Devlin knew this was paramount but saying it and doing it were two different kettles of fish.

The two old partners and buddies chewed the fat for about an hour. Before hanging up, Joe thanked Al for his help. Al responded with a typical "anything for you, Cheech." He also reminded Joe to call on him any time day or night and wished him the best. Joe reiterated his gratitude and settled in for a long night and a longer next few weeks, months.

As Joe entered his squad room, which was a welcome sight after yesterday's field trip to One PP, he was met by the Three Wise Men: Chief of Detectives Harry Brenner, Lieutenant George Moss and FBI Agent and Profiler Russell Hollander. Joe wished them a fairly unenthusiastic good morning and sat down with his coffee mug in one hand and a roll of Tums in the other. Neither Captain Frank Sterling nor Commissioner Ted Fields was present in body, but they were present in spirit. Joe figured one or the other had bent the ear of one or all of them earlier this morning. As Joe was considering which man had received the firmest kick in the posterior, the members of the Task Force started to file in.

This scene reminded Joe of the first day of Catholic school

where students would arrive with shirts pressed, pencils sharpened and shoes shined. The stakes, however, had grown exponentially since those days. The fear of poor grades and parental disapproval had been replaced by just plain terror. Devlin hoped that all these individuals, brought together from different backgrounds, different agencies and different departments, could work together for a common purpose and goal, and apprehending this maniac before he killed an eleventh individual.

That number pre-supposed that the ten bodies are all connected in some way and to the same perpetrator, and that there were no other "unfound" bodies. Joe's nose told him that they were looking for a white male in his thirties or forties, but his nose could not yet determine if there were more than ten victims already, nor when number eleven would be found.

Joe finished off his java, popped the antacids into his mouth and made his way to the Command Center, a room within the precinct that was designated for the Joint Task Force. Not exactly the lobby at the Plaza, but it would suffice for its purpose. He introduced himself, welcomed everyone, made some introductions and began to detail their mission. The first item on Joe's agenda was to summarize Russell Hollander's briefing from yesterday for those not in attendance at the One PP Yukfest.

Upon finishing, he took the opportunity to thank Hollander for giving so generously of his time and expertise for this investigation. Joe figured there was no harm in getting off on the right foot with the FBI, and no reason not to begin with good feelings. Besides, Hollander was an ace (as Al would say) and Joe knew it. He was a key player due to his vast experience and willingness to share information, which was a trait not always possessed by the Feds (or the state or locals, for that matter).

"Since all of the D.O.A.s were from the world of sex and drugs," Joe continued, "we'll begin our search there. Get out on the streets, reach out to your people, your C.I.s. We need to get the ball rolling. Talk to the known prostitutes and dealers. Let them know the importance of a name, of a lead, which they could trade for money or a get-out-of-jail-free card.

"While I expect this to be a cooperative effort, I'll make the crucial decisions and interview the killer once in custody. Obviously, Brenner, Moss and Hollander will play an integral part in this process, up to and including capture."

They nodded in agreement.

"In closing, Commissioner Fields has conveyed to me how desperate the NYPD is to catch this murderer, who has been dubbed the 'Period Killer' because he arrives once a month. Make no mistake about it, we have a sense of urgency, starting now."

On that note, the orientation came to an end. Joe spoke for longer than he had expected but he didn't want to leave any stone unturned. What Joe didn't address was what the consequences were if the Task Force was unsuccessful, if more bodies turned up, if the public's panic turned into anger at law enforcement. The commish was a big supporter of Devlin, but not at the expense of his own career and legacy (not to mention pension). Joe suddenly got a vision of himself in a matching rent-a-cop hat and vest, patrolling suburban shopping mall parking lots.

Chapter 12

The Three Wise Men were the first to exit. Joe figured they were due at NYPD headquarters to meet with either Captain Sterling or Commissioner Fields, or perhaps both. *Better them than me.*

Joe didn't realize that Detectives Lempert and Turner, who were partnered up in Queens homicide, had left the room. They hurriedly re-entered and approached him.

"What's up, guys?"

"We just heard from one of our C.I.s, Detective Lempert said. "He claims that a guy named Malcolm Sturgess was one of the last people to see Tracy Wetherly alive. We were investigating her death as a single. We now believe she was the eighth victim of our perp. She was a prostitute and heroin user. Sturgess apparently was a suspect in the murder of two prostitutes a few years back. Those cases were never closed."

"Also," said Detective Turner, "our C.I. says that an escort he conducts business with claimed that Sturgess was connected to another victim. It turns out his mother was a prostitute and a junkie who Sturgess found dead with a needle in her arm when he was in high school. This Sturgess is half a pimp, too."

Joe was excited to hear this news. "Maybe we caught a break already?" he thought. He had to temper his enthusiasm somewhat as he'd been down this Yellow Brick Road before. Still, it was a start. He shoved his hands into his pockets and stared at the ceiling.

His eyes turned back to his detectives. "Ok, that's good, guys. We need to have a conversation with this Sturgess. Do you know where to grab him up?"

"Yeah, we have an address," Detective Lempert said.

"Fine. Take some back-up from the Task Force and bring him here."

"You got it."

With that the two detectives left. Maybe this was a lead. Maybe it was a dead end. Or if Sturgess wasn't the culprit, perhaps he might have some other names.

Joe slid open a drawer and removed a fresh legal pad. He jotted down notes about the case. Not only what Lempert and Turner had just shared with him but other salient points as well.

After summarizing the conversation about Malcolm Sturgess, he wrote down that none of the victims were moved from a different location. *So he does not touch them in any way. He somehow gets their attention and then they are shot, left at the scene, and our guy leaves on foot. One partial shoe print was found at one scene. But we don't know if he meets up with another guy at a different location who drives them away or if he has a car waiting for him at another location and he drives himself away. Or, he could be on foot the entire time.*

Joe turned the page and on the next fresh sheet of yellow paper noted that it seemed like the killer had a detailed knowledge of law enforcement techniques, which had helped him avoid detection.

An hour later Detectives Lempert and Turner walked into the command center with Malcolm Sturgess between them. He wore black leather pants, a red button-down shirt with a few of the top buttons unbuttoned and a moth-eaten jacket. His fake Rolex peeked out from his left sleeve. *Probably bought on a street corner near Times Square,* Joe surmised. The suspect was ushered into a small interrogation room with a jail cell in the rear.

"Take a seat, Mr. Sturgess," Joe said. The detective sat on the opposite side of the gray metal table from him. Lempert and Turner stood behind Sturgess, leaning against the wall with their arms folded.

Joe rested his hands on the table. "I'm Detective Devlin, Mr. Sturgess. Do you know why you're here?"

He turned behind him and pointed. "These two five-ohs said something about Tracy Wetherly. I knew her, yeah." Sturgess raised his voice. "But I didn't have nothing to do with what happened to her."

"Take it easy. We're just gathering facts, conducting interviews and forming timelines."

Sturgess scratched his nose. "You got the wrong guy. I wasn't even in Queens the night she was killed. I was in Manhattan tending to some business."

"And what business are you in?" Joe asked.

"I'm sort of an entrepreneur. I'm a self-starter."

Detective Lempert said, "Cut the crap. We know what you are and what you do. You're freakin' lucky they didn't hang the murders of the two dead prostitutes on you a few years back. What's the matter, Sturgess, you hate junkies and whores because your mom was both?"

Joe held up both hands. "Ok, let's just settle down and take this one step at a time."

Sturgess plastered a smile on his face. "Your boy needs to chill, Detective. Like I told you, I ain't got nothin' to do with that. I was in the West Village, in Washington Square Park that night. I can give you the names of my associates who saw me."

"Yeah, give us a list of your hookers and drug buyers," said Detective Turner.

Joe cringed. He wished these two could keep their pots from boiling over. "How did you know Ms. Wetherly?" he asked. "We're not vice. This is a murder investigation. I need the truth. Now!"

"Ok, Detective, that's cool. Can we be alone, can we dismiss Starsky and Hutch?"

Joe leaned back and put his hands behind his head.

"Detectives, please give us a moment." They mumbled as they exited.

Joe said, "We're alone now, Malcolm. This isn't a reunion. If I don't have some answers in the next five seconds I'm gonna throw you in that cage and leave you there."

"I hear you. Solid. I knew Tracy. She was my employee, if you catch my drift. She was a good earner. Helped me with some petty BS drug stuff too. I didn't know she got shot until the next day. I swear, Detective. I was in the park dealing with my vocation."

"You mean just plain dealing. What about the dead prostitutes Detective Lempert mentioned? And another victim, Sid Harris?"

"Yeah, I knew them from around." Sturgess tapped his foot. "Our worlds kinda…intersect. You know what I mean, or I wouldn't be here, and you know all about me. Finding my mom dead screwed me up. But I wouldn't kill nobody."

"You were one of the last people to see Ms. Wetherly alive, if not the very last."

"Hold up, Detective. I probably saw her earlier that day. I don't keep a tight calendar on my i-Phone. But I didn't see her that night at all."

"Do you know anybody that might be involved? Have you heard anything at your 'office'?"

"No, I'd tell you if I did. I don't know anything." His shoulders sagged.

"What, what is it?" Joe asked. "You can speak freely here."

"Well, a lot of cops come around to break up our activities. Some want to keep the streets clean; some want a little taste for themselves."

Joe adjusted his tie. "Go on."

"Look, I've seen a lot of cops in the areas where they've found some bodies. There's all kinds of freaky shit goin' on there. Sex, drugs, you name it. It's dark and remote. I'm not pointing any fingers. Just saying.

"I hear you. Could you ask around a little? It could be beneficial to you," Joe said.

"Beneficial how?"

"Money."

"10-4. I'll do some checking. But I'm not looking for a suicide mission here. If I finger the fuzz I'll wind up in the trunk of a car headed for a chop-shop in the Bronx."

Joe extended a card to Sturgess. "Call me right away if you have any info. It'll stay between us. If you're straight I won't jam you up. But if you're not the car ride to the Bronx will be the least of your worries. Alright. For now, you can go. I have your cell number. What's your home number?"

"There's a little mix-up with the phone company at present," Sturgess said. "The cell's it right now."

"Don't take any trips. Be reachable. If I need you and can't get you, that'll disappoint me. I may get unpleasant."

"Hey, Detective, no problem. Done."

"You're an ok guy for a five-oh."

"That thought enriches my life. Thanks. I'll be in touch. Stay out of trouble."

Sturgess exited with Joe following a few seconds later. He walked over to Detective Lempert. "Put a squad car on his place. Have his activities tracked. Report back to me. My buddy in IT is installing a monitoring app so we can check his cell phone and computer activity. And take it down a notch next time. There may be a time to exert some force, but we're not there yet. We may not be there at all. Get on it."

"Will do, Joe. No problem. We're on it."

Joe swayed on his feet. He wasn't sure what to do next. His mind was racing in all directions. His cell phone rang and he quickly jolted the receiver to his ear. "Detective Devlin."

"Hi Detective, I'm calling about the serial killer. I heard about him on the news. I live in Queens, not far from where the last body was found. I think I may have seen someone in that area around the time of the murder. My wife objects to me smoking in the house and I sometimes wander over there.

I didn't get a real good look, but I may be able to identify the guy if I saw him again."

Joe knew the area where the last body was found was notorious for drug dealing and sex participation. Those were the activities that this man's wife probably objected to more than the smoking. "What's your name, sir?"

"Gary Carpenter."

"Mr. Carpenter, can you come down to the precinct, the 115, look at some photos and make a statement?"

"Sure. I'll be there in about an hour."

"Thanks, see you then."

Joe hung up the phone, summarized the call to his men, and waited on the arrival of possible witness Gary Carpenter. This could be an early break, or it could be that Mr. Carpenter was a publicity seeker, thought there was money in it for him, or was a crackpot!

Chapter 13

An hour later, Joe pulled into a parking spot abutting the Flushing River, next to a gray and rust colored Ford Taurus. Gary Carpenter had called back to advise Joe that he preferred to have his first meeting at a neutral location. *First meeting?*

Joe had checked some background on this potential witness following his second call to the precinct. Carpenter had expertise in web technologies and databases, and was employed at a small firm in the Kew Gardens section of Queens. Joe found it odd that he had worked at five firms in the last seven years.

Carpenter emerged from his car to greet Joe. He was dressed in jeans and an untucked and unwashed black shirt. His black hair was slicked back and he had stubble on his face.

"Hi, Detective Devlin, I'm Gary Carpenter. It's a real pleasure."

"The pleasure's mine, Mr. Carpenter. Thanks for contacting us."

"Gary, please. And I'm happy to do it."

"Ok, Gary. I don't want to appear rude, but I'd like to get right to it. On the phone you said that you'd observed someone in the area near where the last body was found."

"Yes. I did. As I told you I sometimes walk in that area in the evening. My wife forbids smoking in the house. On the evening in question, I was engaged in a conversation with a man I'd met on my walk, but was distracted by a figure I saw running away."

"I'm not looking to jam you up, Gary, but were you

involved in a drug deal with the man you met up with?"

"Certainly not, Detective. And I didn't meet up with him. Our paths just happened to cross. As we were talking, I saw someone dressed all-in black run from behind an abandoned building. The next day I read in the paper about the lady who got killed in that area and put two and two together."

"Did you get a good look at the person running, other than being dressed in black. Anything that you can remember at all?"

"No, it was dark out. But here's the weird thing. About an hour or so before, I walked past someone on Roosevelt and 108th Street, near a gas station. He had his head down and moved very quickly. It wasn't completely dark yet, so I got a good look at his face, black clothes and black hat."

"And you think that it could be the same individual who ran from behind the building an hour or so later?"

"It could be, Detective." I figured it was worth reporting."

"Agreed. But one thing, Gary. Roosevelt and 108th is a little far from your house. Between strolling there and talking to your friend near the murder scene, I'd say you were out for more than just a nicotine fix."

"Ok, Ok. So I'm not the husband of the year. You'd leave the house for hours too if you had a wife like mine. And yes, I've transacted some business in that area. But that's baby stuff. Do you want this guy or not?"

"Point taken. But could you give me a description based upon your observations when he passed you on the street?"

"Here's where we get into an awkward area," Gary said. "This will hit close to home. I think I recognized him from a local bar that I frequent. He comes in with some pals after softball games. They play darts and guzzle beer. They wear shirts with NYPD stitched on them."

Joe tilted his head to one side. "Could he be on the team but not be a cop? Like maybe he's a friend or just a ringer?"

"I'm not looking for trouble here. But I've heard him talk to the bartender Gil, who's a retired cop. I've heard the war stories. He's a sergeant. I've seen him a few times, but I don't know his name. But Gil does."

Joe stroked his chin and looked out over the water. "If you saw his picture you definitely could ID him?"

"Yeah, sure. And like I said Gil's friendly with him. He might not want to roll on one of his brethren, though."

"Let me worry about that," Joe said. "I'll need you to come down to the precinct. Then I'll pay a visit to see this Gil. What's the name of the tavern?"

"Duffy's Pub. It's sort of a cop hangout."

"What attracted you to that particular bar?"

"One of the waitresses. My wife makes Cruella de Vil look like an animal lover."

Joe forced a smile. "Can you come down now?"

"Can we make it tomorrow, Detective? I'm involved in a matter of national interest where my presence is paramount."

"Excuse me, Gary."

"I'm loathe to share this, but since you're a member of law enforcement I'm comfortable with it. I'm involved with a group of freedom fighters in a coup attempt to oust President Benitez of Paraguay."

Joe's eyes widened. He thought he had a direction to travel, but now his trip was being derailed.

"Is that a fact, Gary? Well, I won't hold you up any longer. Good luck in your mission."

"Thank you, Detective. I'll be in touch soon. Thank you for your courtesy. I'd like to repay your kindness and offer you the opportunity to invest in my uranium field."

Joe shifted from one foot to he other. "Your uranium field?"

Gary picked a piece of lint from his sleeve. "Please, not so loud. Yes, close to Peter Luger's Steakhouse in Brooklyn. I can't guarantee the rate of return but Wall Street is very optimistic. And the uraniam may be needed for a nuclear weapon. Remember I explained about my plans in Paraguay?"

Joe was playing with his cell phone, wishing that Brenner had picked up the call from Gary. "I recall, yes. Like I said, thanks for contacting me and all the luck."

Gary tipped his cap, although he wasn't wearing one, got back into his George W. Bush era car and drove off.

Joe's stare stayed on the car as it exited the parking lot. He considered calling his friend at the State Department to warn of a possible coup in South America, but dismissed the idea. He began to laugh, partly to keep from crying. Part of the day may have been wasted by Gary Carpenter. However, with both Gary's car exhaust and words still hanging in the air, Joe couldn't summarily dismiss this potential lead. Despite Mr. Carpenter's delusions and potential future as a Minister in the Paraguay Cabinet, the detective was wrestling with having to check out Duffy's Pub.

Just to satisfy his curiosity, the detective called his friend with the State Liquor Authoritry, who told Joe that Duffy's Pub is a fairly successful establishment located on the border of Flushing and North Corona. Further, added Joe's pal, it was well known as a place cops regularly frequent.

Chapter 14

Jim awoke to an alarm that went through his head like a nail. He peered at the alarm clock and tried to extricate his left arm, which was trapped under Anakin's massive chest. Finally, after coaxing the Rottweiler to the bottom of the bed with a little sweet talk, he slammed on the snooze button for a few more minutes of rest. Last night Jim had returned home following a walk, then tossed and turned for hours with thoughts of work, Thanksgiving, and his parents visit from Florida.

Eventually, Jim gave in to the reality that he couldn't be late. Today was the Tuesday before Thanksgiving and he had a lot to wrap up at the office, as he'd be off until Monday. He'd taken off extra time to pick up his parents at the airport and his firm was closed the day after the holiday, when shoppers rushed stores as soldiers had rushed Normandy Beach.

He rolled onto his back, fixated on the ceiling and his parents upcoming visit. The telephone conversation he had with his mom last month was still fresh in his mind.

"Why can't you come to Florida this year for Thanksgiving, Jim?" she'd asked. "The weather is great and your dad doesn't look forward to traveling anymore. Also, you guys have that awful serial killer up there. We saw a whole special on him on CNN."

"We went through this last year, Mom," Jim reminded her. "It's not that I don't care about Dad's feelings, and it's not that I don't enjoy my turkey and stuffing in an air-conditioned condo while it's 95 degrees outside. As for the serial killer, we'll safe because the murders have all been in

Queens. Maybe the taxes on Long Island are to high for the killer to afford both a nice home and a nice gun. Taking an Uber from Queens is too expensive!”

“I don't need the sarcasm, young man,” his mom said. “It's not unreasonable for parents to expect their children to visit occasionally, even big shot attorneys.”

“I'm just kidding, Mom,” Jim had said apologetically. “'I'd probably have to take off that entire week, and my work schedule is really a bear around that time. It'll be all I can do just to take off Wednesday. Also, I can't put Anakin on a plane and I don't want to be away from him for an entire week. I know that may seem odd to Dad and you since you guys never had a pet, but it's how I feel.”

“No, I do understand,” his mom said in an accepting tone. “I know how important he is to you. But he's not a substitute for a meaningful relationship. Honey, we worry about you. Are you seeing anybody right now?”

Jim let out a sigh and an ugh that could be heard all the way down the coast. “Mom, let's fight one battle at a time. We can play the Dating Game when you and Dad come to New York. Can we just agree that I'll host Thanksgiving this year? To make you both feel at home, you can cook the turkey and any sides you desire, and Dad can snooze in my recliner after dinner with his belt open. Now is that a deal or what?”

“Ever since you were a boy, James,” his mom said with a good-hearted laugh, “I could never stay mad at you and you could always make me laugh. Both of you boys always could.” Her voice trailed off.

“Hey, Mom,” Jim said in an upbeat tone, “I'll make that dessert for you, the one that you love, the apple crisp, and Michelle will be here, too. I saw her over the weekend, and she can't wait to see you and Dad. On Friday night I'll take you guys to the seafood restaurant we went to last year where you picked out the biggest lobster in the tank. I may even pay!”

The sound of his mother's laughter on the other end of the

phone made Jim smile and tear up. He loved her so much.

"Okay, Mr. Attorney, you won your case. You've convinced the jury. Now all I have to do is convince your dad."

Several hours later Jim's mom called to say that his father had agreed to spend the holiday in New York and was looking forward to the trip. Jim felt that maybe his mom had dressed up his dad's response with the inclusion of the idea that he was looking forward to travelling, but nevertheless Jim was pleased and relieved.

Jim kicked off the covers and rolled out of bed, heading downstairs with a happy and hungry dog at his heels. After Anakin was fed and let out, Jim sat down to coffee, two scrambled eggs and the newspaper. He'd missed the late news.

Jim stared at the headline in today's paper without blinking. His mouth slowly dropped open. It read, "11th Victim Found in Queens." The article said that a police officer and his dog on a routine training exercise had found the body of Maureen Carter in a small piece of brush. She'd been killed by a single gunshot to the head. According to the story, Carter was a struggling mother who worked as a prostitute to help pay the mortgage.

Jim's lower lip quivered, and he felt a twisted lump in his throat. He thought of her kids having to hear the news that their mother had been killed and her body left to rot in some isolated area. Especially depressing was the fact that this incident occurred just two days before the holiday.

As Jim buttered his toast, he was struck by the thought that Maureen Carter's children would come to figure out what he had learned. Following the death of a loved one, perhaps even more so if it's a violent death, the holidays would be transformed from a time of celebration to sad days filled with increased irritability and maudlin thoughts. Each holiday would be a trigger for depression.

Just the anticipation of his parents' arrival tomorrow and Thanksgiving the day filled Joe with angst and a sense of increased pressure. It's not that he didn't love them. Quite the opposite. But as he once told his psychiatrist, Jim feared the ruminating that occurred over holidays would push him over the edge. He knew he had to be a support system for his parents but wondered who would perform the same task for him. He'd asked for guidance from Dr. Lawrence on how to keep it together.

The doctor had tried to comfort Jim by teaching him coping mechanisms and relaxation techniques. Dr. Lawrence stressed walking, reading a light-hearted book, meditating and being around good friends. Jim experienced minimal success when attempting these endeavors.

The thought of his mom falling apart at the mention of David was bringing on a panic attack. Jim had to set down his cup of coffee and wipe his sweaty brow with his napkin. He pushed his plate with the half-eaten eggs away as he felt nausea approaching. Jim closed his eyes, resting his head in his hands.

This downward spiral was halted by the loud sound of Anakin, who was fidgeting outside the sliding glass back door. Saved by the bell, or the Rottweiler in this case. Jim hustled to let him in, feeling a bit more stable. He took a last swig from his coffee mug and raced upstairs to get ready for his train into Manhattan.

Chapter 15

Jim sat quietly in the waiting area at JFK Airport. He was nursing a second cup of coffee and thumbing through a magazine. Normally, to kill a little time, he'd take out his phone and view some texts or e-mails, but he wasn't in the mood for technology. Jim chose to do some reading from a magazine instead, as he waited for his parents plane to arrive from Florida.

The airport was packed with holiday travelers. Jim looked up to glance at the volume of people hustling to get to their destination. He'd hoped that his parents would arrive on Tuesday night so he could avoid the bumper-to-bumper traffic that would be waiting for him as he departed the airport and drove home on the Long Island Expressway. The LIE was a parking lot each afternoon during rush hour and today they would make it home sooner hopping on one leg. However, Jim didn't press the issue with his mom, especially since he'd won his argument and would eat his holiday bird in his own home.

Jim re-checked the arrival board and was pleased to see that his parents' flight had just landed. He discarded his coffee cup and magazine and headed toward the area where he'd meet up with them.

As he surveyed the sea of people coming down the corridor to meet their loved ones, Jim finally saw his family. His dad was wearing a satisfied smile and his mom was waving and walking quickly. They met and embraced. His mom held on to Jim very tightly, as if she could hug away her hurt. "It's so good to see you, son."

His dad's blue eyes were bleary. Jim figured it was the

result of a combination of his dislike of travel and the idea that only one son could meet them at the airport. Edward's skin appeared leathery; his receding hairline more pronounced. He was still barrel-chested, but Jim noticed the barrel now reached his stomach. His dad had aged much more than the five months since his last visit. But his strong hands felt good as they patted Jim's back.

"It's great to see you, Jim."

"You, too, Dad, how was the flight?"

"Oh, not bad."

"Yes, not bad, Jim," his mom said. "As soon as we landed your dad stopped praying."

His mom's round amber eyes left Jim for a moment, moved to Edward as they shared a laugh, and returned to meet Jim's. His mom was petite, with short raven hair and smooth, bronzed skin. Physically, she had aged better than her husband, but Jim knew her soul was as shattered as the vase she'd smashed when they returned from David's funeral.

After exchanging kisses and pleasantries, the three gathered up the luggage and soon were headed to Jim's house.

Jim's SUV provided plenty of room for its three occupants and the luggage. His dad occupied the passenger seat because he got car sick while riding in the back. His mom rode in the back seat happily as seeing her son was enough to bring a smile to her face.

While they were sitting in the nightmarish traffic Jim had anticipated, they made the obligatory small talk. Edward filled Jim in on the comings and goings in their Tampa condo community. The usual stuff; who was sick, who was dying and who had just died. Jim was not aware of most of the names and places Edward was discussing, but he let his dad talk.

As Edward wrapped up his state of Florida address, his mom took the baton and ran with it. Phyllis filled Jim in on any detail Edward may have missed.

"Rich and Barbara dropped us off at the airport and send their best. They hope to see you at Christmas. Barbara's daughter will be visiting them. Barb said she'd love to see you. You remember Allison. The tall pretty blonde. What a nice girl. She just became the principal of her school."

Jim stared ahead and just smiled. He couldn't blame his mom for not wanting him to be alone. He proceeded to fill his parents in on his life. "Not much different than when I saw you guys back in June. Nothing's really changed. Work is the same. I have a large caseload but a good team around me. My boss Bill Dunn's excellent guy. You remember him from the funeral, right?

"Yes, of course I do," Jim's dad said. "A real nice man, very kind and compassionate. You hate to meet people under those circumstances. I was such a mess, so out of it, we all were. But Mr. Dunn let me vent and wanted to hear about David."

"I remember him, too," Jim's mom said. "He came back to the house, had food delivered, too."

As Jim reached the exit before his, his dad shifted in his passenger seat. Jim knew that meant either Edward had a prostate or colon condition that made comfortable sitting a chore, or more likely that his dad was preparing to ask him a question.

"You stated earlier," he said in his usual serious fashion, "that not much has changed since we were here five months ago. I assume that was meant in regard to your law practice, and of course, Anakin.

"But there has been some rather distressing news and events in your area recently. We've read and seen the details of the so-called 'Period Killer,' if you'll excuse my being indelicate. Ten people killed in Queens alone, and an eleventh victim found this week. Your mom didn't really want you to know about our concern, but I assured her that you'd understand."

Edward was forever making strong points and arguments

that Jim couldn't counter. His dad was never unfair, overly emotional, unreasonable or condescending. So how could Jim argue with parental worry? They'd suffered so much. Jim couldn't muster any argument or opposing point.

"I completely get it," Jim said. "I realize it's fruitless to assure you two how safe I feel and how careful I am at all times. Nobody can blame a parent for worrying about their children, especially you guys. But trust me, they will catch this guy soon and some sense of normalcy will return to the city."

"Okay, Counselor," said his mom. "You win. We'll still worry, but we'll also do our best to keep our anxiety on a leash."

As Jim began to slow down to turn off at his exit, his mom moved up slowly from her seat behind Edward to address Jim. "I'm glad we got that stuff off our chests. Your dad and I talked about something on the plane and I want to see how you feel about it."

Jim held his breath. An open-ended parental concern could be almost anything.

"Is it too much to ask our son to come down to Tampa to celebrate Christmas with his parents?"

Ugh. Jim knew that he'd be cornered this weekend, but he had anticipated the subject popping up on Friday or Saturday. This Wednesday, pre-Thanksgiving sneak attack was a parental special. Attack the enemy when they least expect it and are the most vulnerable. He assumed his mom had gotten this tactic from Sun Tzu's *The Art of War*.

If he had to make an argument to a jury to convince them that he shouldn't have to travel to the sunshine state he'd lose. He'd spent one Christmas in Florida and felt that a ninety-degree day didn't make for a traditional or joyous Yule Tide. However, he was running out of excuses and didn't want to hurt his parents' feelings.

"We'll see," he said.

He figured this would buy him some time. This was how

his parents had responded to his childhood questions and requests. It was an effective tool for his mom and dad and he hoped for the same level of success with it.

"What I mean is, I need to see my court calendar and what kind of a workload I have over the next few weeks. I'll have to let you know."

"It would mean a lot to your mother, and to me as well," his dad said. "We'd love for you to spend the week at our condo, spend some time in the sun and see some of our friends. And you could spend some time with Barbara's daughter Allison. It would make for a great Christmas, and save us another plane trip."

Jim's house was approaching, and he didn't want this issue to linger. He wanted his parents to have a relaxing weekend.

"Okay, sounds like a plan," he said. "I'll check flights over the weekend, and we'll make it work. I'll ask my neighbors to watch Anakin. The O'Connors have watched him before, and it went well. Their kids love Anakin.

The O'Connors, Sheila and Tom, occupied the house between Jim and Det. Devlin. Jim considered them good neighbors and friends. They were funny and entertaining, battling more than Ali and Frazier, yet had created a loving home for their kids. Tom was a mild-mannered guy while Sheila stressed over what time the ice cream truck would pass by.

"It shouldn't be a problem. I'll load up on sunscreen, Mah Jongg tiles and air sick bags."

Phyllis and Edward shot each other a look and a smile. "Thanks for not giving us a hard time," mom said, "and it's nice to see my boy's still a wise ass!"

Chapter 16

Jim was awoken on Thanksgiving morning by his mom, who cheerfully opened his bedroom door at eight o'clock with a happy holiday greeting and an announcement that breakfast was ready. Suddenly, he had a flashback to high school. He glanced around the room to make sure that his book bag was not resting on the chair in the corner. When fully awake, the realization that his briefcase was on the floor and Anakin was on the bed relieved him. Jim remembered from their prior visit that their Florida schedule didn't exactly match his New York timetable. Phyllis coaxed Anakin out of the bed and took him downstairs, while reminding Jim not to be too long or his eggs would get cold.

Jim was greeted at the breakfast table by a "Look who's up" from his dad and a hearty "good morning" from his mom. The tabled was adorned with eggs, toast, bacon, orange juice and coffee. Jim expressed his appreciation to his mom for fixing a delicious breakfast, a sentiment seconded by Edward.

Phyllis thanked them, took a sip of coffee, and then stared at the empty fourth chair at the breakfast table. Jim assumed that she was thinking that the holidays were a reminder that they'd never be a family of four again, that David's absence was permanent. She tried to speak, but instead got choked up and ran into the bathroom.

Jim recalled the night before David's wake. His parents were staying with him, and he passed by the guest room. The door was ajar. His right hand pushed at the door to reveal his mom staring at his brother's high school graduation photo. She was in a trance-like state, her words muffled by sobs and ragged breathing. The next day, his mom would have to walk into a funeral home and see her baby boy lying in a box.

The next sound they heard was the faucet running at full blast, with his mom's sobs muffled by the running water. "Damn, damn," she shouted. The two men sat in silence. His dad's face was expressionless, yet spoke volumes, and Jim was caught between staying planted in his chair and racing to comfort his mom. The deafening silence was broken by his mom, who emerged from the bathroom with swollen eyes, puffy cheeks and a tissue balled up in one hand.

"Sorry, guys, it just came over me all of a sudden." Her hands were shaking. "That happens sometimes, and I feel like I'm trying to hold back the ocean with a broom. I remember how much David loved holidays, loved being with his family. A couple of years he was late to dinner because he would serve meals at the shelter. Oh my God."

"We understand, Phyllis," Jim's dad said, standing up to hug his wife. "And we love you."

"Sure we do, Mom." Jim's placed his left hand assuredly on her right arm.

Shortly after breakfast, Edward settled into a recliner and Jim rubbed his dog's head as they both occupied the couch.

"Your mother tells me that Michelle will be over this afternoon," his dad said.

Anakin lifted his head at the mention of Michelle's name.

"She'll be here," Jim said. "I spoke to her on Monday. She's really looking forward to it. She regretted not getting a chance to see you two the last time you visited."

"How's she doing?" Edward asked.

"Mixed. A lot of terrible days. She's a tough lady with a strong will, but there are days when it really gets to her."

"I hope she knows your mom and I are always there for her, anytime she needs." Edward began to tear up a little, surprising Jim. "She's still my daughter-in-law, always will be. Your mother feels the same way."

Jim was now fighting back tears. David's name always came up during any family gathering. Sometimes Jim was unable to shut out the memories, and they came flooding back to him at those moments.

Jim fought to compose himself using a method Dr. Lawrence had taught him. He regulated his breath, breathing in deeply through his nose, then gradually letting the air escape through his pursed lips. "You know I feel the same way. We keep in touch and have dinner on occasion."

Edward said, "She's a very special person. A wonderful wife and nurse, plus all her volunteering, charity work and fund-raising. Her family's great, too. They were a great source of support for your mom and me." Jim's dad dabbed at his eyes with a handkerchief then returned it to his pocket. "Anyway, we're pleased that she'll be over."

"I expressed my appreciation to Michelle when we spoke earlier this week," said Jim, hoping to cheer up his dad. "She said she wouldn't miss this opportunity to visit with you and mom. I also invited over her parents, but they had made other plans. Michelle assured me that her parents would stop over before you guys go back to Florida."

"Good," Edward said. "I'm looking forward to seeing them."

Jim's recalled the day they heard about David's death. Michelle had called him around 10:30 p.m.

"David was supposed to be home by 7:30 p.m. He told me he had to work a little later tonight. He was in the office today, not on-site. I've called him a lot and it goes straight to voice mail. I've tried some of our friends, but they haven't seen him. You know him, he's never late. I'm worried."

"Okay, Michelle, I'm sure he's fine. But keep trying. I'll be right over."

David and Michelle lived in the same Long Island county, a fifteen-minute drive away. Michelle looked pale white as she answered the door. "Still nothing. Did you hear anything?"

"No. Are you sure he didn't say he was going somewhere or doing something tonight?"

"He just said he'd be home around 7:30. I called the construction office, but nobody answered. I have a bad feeling, Jim."

So did he, but he thwarted his face from revealing that. "Let's sit for a minute. I'll make you some tea."

They sat talking for about an hour until Jim's cell phone rang. He prayed it was David, but it was a member of his softball team, Rich Donnelly. The call wouldn't have alarmed Jim except for the fact that Rich was a detective in Queens homicide. Jim's heart sank.

"Hi, Rich,"

"Hi, Jim. Are you at home?"

"No, I'm at David's house. Michelle and I can't reach him."

"Yeah, that's what we need to talk about. I'll be right over."

Michelle's cell phone rang, and she apologized to her friend that she couldn't talk now. A few seconds later Michelle's mom called, and they spoke briefly.

The doorbell rang a moment later. Michelle opened the door to find Detective Donnelly standing meekly under the porch light. She let out a harsh wail, "Oh, no, oh please God no." Her chest heaved unevenly. She turned deathly pale and looked like she was going to faint, so Jim and Rich helped her to the couch.

"I'm so sorry, Michelle. He was a terrific guy," said the detective.

Michelle fell into Jim's lap, crying hysterically. "Why, Jim, why, he was such a kind person? Rich, what happened to David?"

"Our best guess is that someone pulled a gun on him in the company parking lot and tried to rob him. David probably fought back and was shot in the chest. There's been a lot of drug activity and robberies in that wooded area behind that lot. It's dark and isolated around 7:00, 7:30. I'm so sorry. I'm so very sorry. We're gonna get this bastard."

Jim was in total shock. His body went numb. Disoriented, he looked around the room to remember where he was. Jim then heard Michelle was sobbing uncontrollably, her face buried in her hands on his lap. Jim stroked her hair with his hand.

Jim nodded to show Rich he appreciated his thoughts. He was fighting the urge to scream or punch the wall, and fighting his dinner, which was rising in his digestive tract toward his throat.

As Rich said good-bye, Michelle lifted her head. "You know Rich, if the guy would've just asked David for money, he'd have given it to him. That's the way he was."

"I know he was, Michelle. I know. I'm sorry for your loss. Take care. Please let me know if you need anything. I'll be in touch."

The sound of the door closing triggered another outburst from Michelle. "I loved him so much, Jim, and he loved you so much. Christ, what am I going to do? How are we going to tell your parents?"

Jim's head was spinning, and he was trying to keep it together for Michelle. To keep from crying, he bit his lip so hard that he could taste drops of blood on his tongue.

"You need to rest, Michelle. I know sometimes you take a sleeping pill. Tonight, take two and then I'll go to my parents."

After Michelle dozed off, Jim covered her with a blanket on the couch and drove to his parents' house. A minute into the drive he began to cry loudly, wiping the tears away. When he returned his left hand to the steering wheel, his right hand banged uncontrollably on the dashboard. Jim let out a scream, "Noooo…."

He'd never dropped by his parents' house after midnight before. He stood in the shadow of the door before pressing the bell. He tried to rehearse what he'd say but failed. The sound of the bell would jolt his parents awake and scare them. He closed his eyes and rang it.

A minute later the upstairs light went on, and his mom was putting her robe on, gingerly negotiating the stairs, his dad a step behind. Peering through the glass door, Jim's eyes met his mom's, and he saw his mom's expression change. She unlocked the door and flung it open. Jim stood frozen with bloodshot eyes. Every muscle in his body was tensed. He began to cry.

Her face was wan and pallid. Jim went to her to console her and to hold her up. His mom buried her forehead in his shoulder. She screamed hysterically, "My baby's gone."

Now, his mom entered the room after babysitting their meal. She was repeatedly wringing her hands on a dishtowel and staring hopelessly at the floor. Jim's heart broke for her. "Mom, I can't believe all that you've done. All you need now is a phone booth to change into your cape."

"Thanks. Why are you guys sitting in the house? Jim, take your father outside for a little fresh air. You could use some yourself."

The two men did some half-hearted stretching and hit the pavement. They weren't outside for two minutes when Edward commented how the cold weather, now that he was a Florida resident, went right through him. It was not a cold day by New York standards, but Edward's thermostat was on Tampa's normal. Jim asked if he wanted to go back inside, but Edward assured him that as he moved he'd warm up.

They ambled along at a slow pace, passing the O'Connor's house and then the corner home, which belonged to the Devlins. Jim had not seen much of Joe lately, since the night that they ran into each other at The Leaning Tower. Jim figured the detective had been tied up with the investigation.

Now, Jim witnessed Joe come out of his house carrying a bag of garbage. He cringed at the thought of asking Joe about the status of the case on a holiday, but he was interested and wanted to help if he could.

"Hello, detective, Happy Thanksgiving."

"Good morning, Jim, same to you."

"This is my dad, Edward Bradley."

Joe put down the bag of garbage, wiped his hands on his sweatpants and extended his hand to Edward. The two men shook hands. "Pleasure to meet you, Mr. Bradley. Happy Turkey Day to you."

"Call me Edward, please, detective, and the same to you."

"Call me Joe, please."

"Sure, glad to meet you, Joe."

"Likewise."

"On cleaning duty?" Jim inquired.

"Yeah," said Joe with a slight chuckle. "My wife likes when I'm out of the kitchen. Actually, I'm goin' for a walk. I took it up a few years ago and now I'm addicted. It helps to balance out my beer drinking and cigarette smoking."

Edward and Jim both laughed.

"Listen, Joe, I just had an idea. Just my parents and my sister-in-law will be over for dinner. Why don't you and your wife join us if you don't have anything special going on?"

"We'd love to have you and your wife over," Edward chimed in. "It's no imposition."

"Thanks. We have no plans. Just Patty and me. We'd planned on a quiet day, but I think it would be good for us. Let me see how she feels, and I'll let you know."

"Sounds like a plan. We usually eat around 2:00 p.m."

"All right, then," said Joe. "Thanks for the invite. It's much appreciated. Give me a few minutes and I'll drop by to let you know, but I think we're good."

"Looking forward to it," Jim said.

They smiled and headed toward their respective homes as if they had just made a dent in solving world peace.

About fifteen minutes later Joe appeared at the Bradley door and asked Jim to come outside for a moment.

"I can't tell you how thoughtful your invitation was. It

really moved my wife. But she's already prepared our dinner. However, we'd love to come over later in the day for dessert if that's okay. Does that work for you?"

"Yeah, sure. Sounds good."

"Should we say around 4:30?"

"Good. See you then."

As Jim came back inside his mom was coming downstairs. He explained what was happening and she inquired about Joe.

"Truthfully, I don't really know him well. We only run into each other now and then. We were just talking and the invitation sort of popped out."

"Well, this is a good day to have a neighbor into your home."

"How can I argue with you, Mom?"

"You can try, but I'll win."

"But you don't play fair."

"That's why I always win."

Chapter 17

At 1:00 p.m. Michelle Wagner rang the doorbell. She'd remained in the area following the death of her husband but moved out of their house into a condo. She told Jim that there were too many memories there and she needed a fresh start. Jim understood. How could he not?

Phyllis ran to the door when she saw it was her daughter-in-law. She hurriedly opened the door to give Michelle a big hug and kiss. Tears filled both women's eyes. Although they kept in touch, they hadn't seen each other since last Christmas.

Edward joined Phyllis at the door and the three embraced. Jim watched from the kitchen. Feeling himself getting choked up, he forced a smile; he didn't want to greet Michelle with a somber expression on his face.

Edward stepped back and said to Phyllis, "Give the lady some air, will you?"

Phyllis wiped away a tear and moved to open up a path for Jim, who greeted Michelle with a strong embrace. He observed, "You look terrific."

Michelle, wiping away a tear of her own, said, "I bet you say that to all your sisters-in-laws. Oh, Jim, I made you an apple pie and for Mom and Dad I made chocolate chip cookies and brownies."

Jim wondered what would happen when and if Michelle were able to move on and meet a new man. That thought filled him with anxiety. *How would his parents react?* At some point she would have to move on with her life, but his parents never would.

As they entered the kitchen, Jim had a flashback to the

evening of the funeral. The family had returned to his house after the burial. At the time, Jim's parents were still living in Nassau County, as were David and Michelle, but Jim thought it best to have everyone at his house. His parents and sister-in-law were in no condition to entertain. Neither was he, but it was the right thing to do.

Jim's mom had come home from the funeral and gone immediately upstairs to the bathroom after not saying a word in the car. His dad sat at the kitchen table, loosened his tie, fussed with his watchband, and stared at the stairs. After about 10 minutes, his mom came down and plopped into a chair.

The living room was her next stop, where she examined each photo Jim had, many with David. She spoke to each picture softly, patting them with one hand, dabbing her eyes with a crushed tissue with the other. His dad followed her into the living room, and was about to hold her when his mom picked up a vase, screamed, "Why, god damn it, why?"

She raised the vase near her right ear and threw it against the wall. The sound of her yell, coupled with the noise of the vase smashing against the wall caused Michelle to run into the room, where the two of them collapsed to the floor.

Jim wanted to clear his mind of this memory. He told Michelle, "My neighbor and his wife will be joining us for dessert. They couldn't make it for dinner but will be here at 4:30."

"Well, that sounds great. I hope I brought enough dessert."

Phyllis chuckled. "Believe me, sweetheart, between me, you and whatever the Devlins bring, we will have enough through the New Year."

Michelle laughed. She turned to Jim. "Where's my beautiful boy?"

"I'm right here," responded Jim.

"Not you, you fool, where's Anakin?"

"He's napping in my bed."

Suddenly, as if he knew he was being discussed, Anakin

rumbled down the stairs, sounding like a combination of Niagara Falls and the *William Tell* Overture. When he made it to the bottom of the stairs, he headed straight for Michelle. "Here's my beautiful boy, here's my strong baby," Michelle repeated as she rubbed his powerful body and smooched his head. Anakin shot a look at Jim as if to say, "By the way, this is how a dog should be greeted and treated!"

After dinner, they made their way from the kitchen to the living room. Michelle insisted on clearing the table and doing the dishes, but Phyllis assured her that Edward and Jim would love to perform those tasks.

Following clean-up duty, Edward sat in Jim's recliner and fussed with his belt buckle. His son figured he was getting ready for a pre-dessert nap. Phyllis and Michelle conversed about the trip up to New York, life in Florida and the goings-on at New York County Hospital, where Michelle worked as a nurse on night duty. Just as Edward had begun to snore the doorbell rang.

Joe and Patricia Devlin were at the door accompanied by desserts. Jim let them in and introduced everyone. Edward made a point of announcing that he'd met Joe earlier in the day. Jim wasn't sure why that was important, unless Edward felt that they'd go bowling together afterward or shoot pool.

Patricia Devlin's brunette hair flowed over her shoulders. She had a shapely figure and was intelligent and dignified in expression. She conveyed her appreciation for the gracious invitation. Joe echoed her sentiment.

"I wasn't sure what everybody liked," said Patricia, "so I made an apple pie, a blueberry pie and some cookies."

"That works for us," Edward smiled.

"You didn't have to do that, but it was so thoughtful," said Phyllis.

Jim brought the goodies into the kitchen. Between Phyllis, Michelle and Patricia, they would be eating desserts until Super Bowl Sunday. Following holiday occasions, Jim usually brought some goodies to the office. If it were free, the employees would eat dirty socks.

While everyone was getting acquainted in the living room, Anakin had returned downstairs from another nap. If he had a button on his pants, he would attempt to loosen it. As he entered the room, Joe reached out to pet the welcoming Rottweiler. Joe had met Anakin before as Jim brought him on an occasional walk. Patricia hadn't had the pleasure and her eyes widened as she took in his size.

"Don't worry Mrs. Devlin," Michelle said. "He's a sweetheart, really. He looks tough but he's not aggressive."

"Oh, I can see he's a good boy. At first sight he's just intimidating to look at. And please, call me Patty."

"I know what you mean, Patty," said Phyllis. "When Jim first got him, I was a little skittish around him. But you will see how sweet he is."

Jim had been listening to Anakin's report card and felt like a proud papa.

Phyllis, Patricia and Michelle had formed their own social club, adjourning to the kitchen.

"So, Joe," Edward said, "Jim tells me you're an NYPD Detective. I always had a lot of respect for the police. You guys have a difficult job."

"That's nice to hear, Edward."

"We're reading and hearing a lot down in Florida about this serial killer here in New York. Do you know anything, or have you heard anything about the case or the investigation?'

"Dad, it's Thanksgiving. Let Joe have a day off. He doesn't want to talk shop."

"No, it's okay," stated Joe, leaning forward with his hand up. "Not a problem. It's ironic that you should ask, Edward. I'm the lead investigator on a Task Force assigned to capture this killer. We formed last month and have been working tirelessly since. Patty will tell you this is my first day off in over a month. But our command center is manned as we speak. We're going to get this guy."

"Wow, that's really something," said Edward. "I've been

following this story with interest from afar and now here I am, sitting with the lead investigator. Small world. I'll keep good thoughts on your team, and I always pray for the families. My wife and I know what it's like to lose a child."

Jim was shocked that his dad had told essentially a stranger about David. He was such a private individual, but he just blurted it out.

"Jim told me. Please accept my condolences. That's just horrible." Joe's eyes became watery. "We lost our son a few years ago. Thomas was almost thirteen."

Edward frowned. "We're so sorry for your loss. You and Patty will be in our prayers."

Joe removed a handkerchief from his pocket and dabbed his eyes. Edward excused himself and headed upstairs.

"My dad just needs a minute."

"I hope I didn't upset him."

"Not at all, Joe. Now that we have a moment, how's the investigation progressing."

"I wish I had more positive news Jim. We're running in place a bit, sifting through many false witnesses and phony leads."

"I've heard that becomes a big problem in high-profile cases."

"Yes, it's been an issue. I had a guy call me last month. He was sure he'd spotted a man dressed in black running from the area where the tenth victim had been found. Unfortunately, this 'witness' is involved in a plot to topple a government in Latin America and also asked me to invest in his uranium field near the Brooklyn Bridge."

Jim tried unsuccessfully to hold in his laugh. "Sorry, Joe."

"Don't be. I laugh to keep my sanity. A couple of my detectives got a tip from an informant about a possible suspect. You know, a lifetime in the drugs and sex business. We brought him in, grilled him, monitored his activities, but it yielded nothing. It's time consuming and frustrating. Sorry to vent."

"No, I asked. I appreciate your candor." Jim rubbed his forehead. "I don't want to overstep, but can I ask you a frank question?"

"Sure."

"Well, an editorial I read suggested that the murderer could be connected to New York's finest. Are you guys pursuing that avenue? Again, I hope I'm not infringing on our friendship."

"No, it's fine, Jim. We've heard internal rumblings about that. Certain things do point in that direction, but so far that's been another blind alley."

"I really wish you the best of luck."

"Thanks, Jim, and thanks again for the invite. It's good for us to get out sometimes, especially on holidays."

The ladies came from the kitchen and Edward emerged from upstairs. Phyllis wanted to know if everyone was ready for dessert.

"Just a minute, Mom," Jim answered as he filled wine glasses for his guests. He rose his glass. "To family and friends, especially new friends. May we all see joyous days ahead. We're grateful today for the roof over our head, the food on our table and those with whom we share this special day. We remember the loved ones who are no longer with us, and we wish them, and all of us, peace."

"Here, here," said Joe, with an arm around Patty.

"Well said, son." His dad clicked his glass with Jim's.

"That was lovely," Michelle agreed.

Phyllis cleared a tear and escorted everyone to the dessert table, where they found Anakin camped, snoring.

Chapter 18

Joe Devlin entered Duffy's Pub on a Tuesday morning between Christmas and New Year's. Duffy's was in the North Corona-Flushing area of Queens, a few miles from the detective's precinct. It also had the distinction of being the establishment allegedly frequented by a man that Gary Carpenter had told Joe he'd seen running from an area where a murder occurred. Due to Gary's delusional behavior, Joe was skeptical of his story. But since the investigation wasn't proceeding very well, Joe decided to follow up.

There was a small Christmas tree in the corner to Joe's left, with red and green wrapped boxes beneath it, tied with gold bows. White lights adorned the front of the bar, which was on Joe's right, as well as the outline of the ceiling. The walls were covered with some other holiday knick-knacks, and photographs of local athletes. Directly over the top row of scotch bottles was a picture of the former NYPD commissioner, signed, *To Duff, All the best.*

Behind the bar a heavy-set man wearing a white shirt and a Kelly-green vest was washing shot glasses, then rubbing them dry with a towel draped over his left shoulder. He had thick, silver-gray hair, a snow-white moustache and a round face with watery blue eyes. The bartender turned the water off. He glanced at Joe.

"Sorry, pal, we don't open for another hour."

Joe flashed his badge. "Can you make an exception?"

"For a cop. Anytime."

"Thanks. I'm Detective Joe Devlin. Glad to meet you." Joe extended his hand.

"Likewise. I'm Gil Patterson. Retired Sergeant NYPD."

Gil shook Joe's hand with a strong grip. "What can I do for you, Detective?" Can I get you something to drink?"

"Please call me Joe. No, I'm fine. Thanks. I just need to ask you a few questions. Can I call you Gil?"

"Yes. No problem. Fire away." He placed both hands on the bar and leaned in.

"I'm the lead investigator on a task force assembled to catch the man responsible for multiple murders, many in this area."

"Yes, it's a scary thing, Joe. My wife won't go out at night, and my daughters are in their twenties, but I worry a lot when they're out late. How can I help?"

"Do you know a man named Gary Carpenter?"

Gil stared at the ceiling. "Gary Carpenter. Gary Carpenter." He crinkled his nose and addressed Joe from his peripheral vision. "Squirrely looking dude. Hair slicked back like Pat Riley, always untucked and unshaven. Yeah, I know him. He's given me a few different names. The guy says he needs to conceal his true identity due to his involvement in international global political interests. Don't tell me he's C.I.A"

"No, he's N.U.T.S."

Gil laughed. "Carpenter, or whoever, never paid his tab, so I banned him from the place. What's your interest in him? Is he your guy?"

"No, I don't think that. Currently he's in Paraguay as the acting Minister of paperclips, scotch tape and chewing gum."

Gil's face went blank.

Joe chuckled and held up his left hand. "Just kidding. I need to amuse myself. A few months back Carpenter gave me a story about his involvement in a South America coup attempt and offered me the opportunity to invest in his uranium field in Brooklyn."

Gil slapped the towel against the bar and laughed. "I always knew that guy's elevator didn't go to the top floor. God, that's funny. But I don't get why you're here, Joe."

"Sorry. I'm pussyfooting around. Now, I know he's not credible, to be kind, but this Carpenter guy claims he saw a man running from one of our crime scenes, and that the same man walked past him on the street some hours earlier. Gary says he recognized the man but doesn't know his name. He insists the man he saw is a cop, that he hangs out here and you're friendly with him."

Gil raised an eyebrow. "I want to help, Joe. But I'm not clear who you're talking about. Do you have a description of this guy?"

Joe reached into his inside jacket pocket and pulled out a piece of paper folded in half. He opened it up and handed it to Gil. "After our first meeting, Carpenter came to the 115 and gave this description to a police artist. Again, I know he's not all there, but I need to ask the question. Do you recognize this man, does he resemble anyone you have seen at Duffy's?"

Gil studied the sketch and then began to cough. He removed a handkerchief from his pocket to cover his mouth. "Sorry. Two packs of Camel a day since I was fifteen." The bartender popped a piece of Juicy Fruit gum into his mouth. "It beats Nicorette."

Joe didn't know if Gil was stalling or concerned about identifying this individual. "Does it ring any bells?"

Gil tucked his shirt into pants, wrestled with his belt buckle, which was the flag of Ireland, and smoothed his vest. His white moustache expanded as his face curved into a smile. Then the smile ran away from his face. "I'm sorry, Joe. This is going to be a dead end."

Joe swayed on his feet. "Not sure I understand."

Gil pointed to a spot above some liquor bottles to his left. There was a photo on the wall of a man who looked very similar to the person Gary Carpenter had described to the sketch artist. It hung above New York Yankees and New York Mets pennant flags, and next to a Police Athletic League vintage shield.

"Who is he?" Joe asked.

"My childhood friend and former owner of this pub, Seamus Finnigan Duffy. That picture was taken the Christmas before his untimely death five years ago."

Joe scowled. He slammed his fist down on the bar, disturbing a drying shot glass. He caught one before it fell to the floor and handed it to Gil.

"Sorry. My head said Carpenter was pulling my taffy, but I had to check it out. This bastard wasted parts of three days with his nonsense. I don't know if I'm angry with me or him."

Gil put his right arm on Joe's left arm. "I've been there, Joe. Lots of times. You must chase down any lead, especially on a case like this. Don't beat yourself up."

"Can I beat up Carpenter?" Joe asked.

"Only if you can get past his security at the President's palace."

Joe laughed. Then Gil laughed and filled a glass with seltzer, placing a lemon wedge over the lip. "So your trip here won't be a total loss."

Joe took the glass, raised it up and sipped the cool refreshing beverage. He put a $20 bill on the counter. "Thanks, Gil. For your help, understanding and kindness. Hope to see you again, under better circumstances."

Gil held out the cash for Joe. "Your money's no good here, Detective. It's my pleasure to help a fellow officer."

Joe pointed to Seamus Finnigan Duffy's framed photo. "Make a donation to the Police Athletic League in your pal's name."

"Will do. Thanks Joe. Good luck. Keep in touch."

"I'll do that."

The men shook hands and Joe headed outside. A post-Christmas chill was in the air to match the coldness of the investigation. Joe turned his back to the breeze to light a cigarette. He stood motionless in front of the pub, alternately glaring at the sky and the passing traffic.

It wasn't just the uncertainty of what his next move should be regarding the case that troubled the detective. He also was unsettled about the direction of his career and his life. Each disappointment professionally pulled him farther into his personal abyss.

Joe didn't know how or when he and Patty would ever climb out and see daylight. He had a thought. An idea he'd been mulling over for a while. Now wasn't the time to play that card, as he had a lot of work to do first.

He snuffed out his Marlboro on the bottom of his shoe and threw it in the garbage can in front of a newsstand. Joe rubbed his hands together to warm them up, then headed to his car. The detective badly wanted to think about the future, but there were too many details and tasks that needed to be dealt with and handled in the present

.

Chapter 19

On a late January morning, Joe Devlin sat across from Clayton Taggart in a booth at the Harvest Diner on Jackson Avenue in Queens. Taggart was ex-army and a former Confidential Informant for the detective when he was in the narcotics division. He ceased being Joe's C.I. after a few drug arrests had changed his name to a number in upstate New York.

An hour ago, Taggart had called Joe at the precinct to advise him of two items. First, that he was out of prison. Second, that he might have information regarding the serial killer, who was now responsible for 13 deaths. The task force was not inundated with solid leads, so he agreed to meet his former C.I.

They had just ordered. Joe was studying Taggart's face. "So how are you doing, Clay?"

"How does it look like I'm doin'?"

Fair answer. Taggart was a far cry from the impressive looking person he was at the time of his discharge from the army, after which he'd helped Joe on some drug cases. At that time, he had the build of a man who used his muscle for a living. He was about six feet tall, clean-shaven, with a buzz cut, thick arms and a broad chest. Taggart was also known to be a sharp dresser. But now his unwashed hair had grown past his shoulders, his unruly beard past his chin and his army jacket was worn and tattered.

"Okay, never mind. How long have you been out?"

"About six months. I didn't want to contact you until I got my act together."

This was together? Joe wondered what apart looked like.

"You said you had information for me, like the old days. What have you got?"

"I know who your guy is, your killer!"

"You do, that's good news, Clay. Tell me, who is it?"

"Alex Ortiz."

Joe let out a long, annoyed sigh. "Alex Ortiz. The Queens councilman?"

"No, his son, Alex junior."

Joe knew of Alex junior's past transgressions, including a history of drug offenses and aggressive behavior toward women. His father, Councilman Ortiz, had all these investigations and incidents squashed.

"What makes you think the Ortiz kid is our guy?"

"I heard it from a person I met in the joint upstate. He was up there on some drug stuff. He hangs out at the same place I do."

"You mean he has the same dealer as you?"

"I plead the Fifth, Detective. The point is he and Alex junior went to school together, even were arrested together once."

"But does he know Ortiz is the killer?"

"He claims the two were throwing a few back one night, talking over old times. Ortiz was completely wasted and got abusive with the bartender. The bartender cursed at him, threatened him, and tried to get him thrown out. The kid then pulls out a gun and waves it at the bartender and a bouncer, screaming that they have no idea who they're screwing with. My jail buddy, Everett Michaels figures Ortiz means that his dad's a councilman. But later that night, somewhere in the middle of doing lines and throwing up, the kid tells Everett that he's gonna come back another night and kill those two guys."

Joe got irritated. "Look, Clay, this all sounds interesting, but I don't have time for this crap. I'm too busy watching my career go down the drain."

"Please let me finish. My friend told me that when he

laughed at Ortiz's death threat, the kid goes on to tell him that a lot of people have underestimated him and wish they hadn't, like all those dead whores and dealers you've heard about on the news."

Joe didn't know what to think. "Did your friend see the gun?"

"He never got a good look at it. All hell broke loose when Ortiz started waving it around. Anyway, my friend eggs the kid on, tells him he's full of shit. Ortiz tells him about the first one that was killed, a prostitute. She apparently took his wallet, then called him the next day to say she wanted to return it. When they met up, she threatened to blackmail him. She probably recognized his name and knew he was a councilman's son. It seems she had other clients with political ties. After he agreed to an amount, he started to walk away, then turned back and shot her. He's a marksman, Joe."

"So are you."

"Yes, but I pay for drugs, not sex."

"That's commendable, Clay. Okay, maybe this is true. Maybe he confesses to a lifelong friend in a drunk and drug induced moment. He wants to be feared, he wants to be the big man he never was. I get it. But why tell you?"

"Look, Joe, I'm not a technical advisor on CSI. We were just talking, we had some junk to keep us company, and he tells me this story."

"So why are you now sharing this with me?"

"Before I got turned sideways, I spent time in the army and helping out you cops. I don't know, maybe it's a chance to get my life back. Maybe there's a reward? In any case, I want to do the right thing."

"Yeah, you and Spike Lee."

"So where do we go from here?" asked Taggart.

"*We* don't do anything. *I* will take it from here. This whole thing is probably nonsense. Either your jail pal or you could be yanking my chain, and if so, you'll be freakin' sorry. But right now, I don't have much else, so I will follow up and pursue this 'lead'. Don't do or say anything, I mean anything, about this to anyone else. Do nothing until you hear from me."

"Okay, sure, Joe. Thanks for breakfast. You think you could spot me a few bucks? I haven't been eating so good lately."

"Here's a twenty. Tell your dealer that's all I had on me."

"That's cold, JD, ice cold. But I like you."

"I can face the rest of the day knowing that."

Taggart laughed and arose from his side of the booth, and Joe followed him out the door of the diner. Joe thanked him and watched as his former C.I. made his way down Jackson Avenue, presumably to put Joe's twenty dollars to good use.

Joe was a solitary figure staring into the late morning sky. He changed his gaze to the street sign above, the corner of Jackson Avenue and 48th street. These cross streets reminded Joe that he was now at a crossroads, both in his life and regarding this investigation. As far-fetched as the story he heard was, he could not ignore the possibility that it might be true. On the other hand, this could be a trip to Never-Never land.

The detective simultaneously suspected all three men, and none of them.

Everett Michaels could be the real killer. *Were thirteen murders a big leap for a guy with a drug history*? He obviously could have lied to Taggart about Ortiz's confession. Everett Michaels could also be crazy like Gary Carpenter and think he was a participant in installing a puppet regime in the southern hemisphere.

Clayton Taggart could also have embellished the story, or made it up entirely, to mask the fact that he was the killer. He was an expert with handguns. When he was discharged from the army, he tried to become a cop, but couldn't pass the psych exam. While working with the NYPD he had been sent to prison upstate for several drug offenses. No violent offenses, though. Joe would have to investigate his background in the army, and into his relationship with Everett Michaels.

But why would Taggart come to the guy who was leading the investigation? Joe thought Taggart's behavior could be like arsonists who hang around to see the wreckage, and then want to be involved in the investigation. The old Taggart would never have been capable of any of this, but he hadn't seen the new Taggart much in the last few years, and what he saw today hadn't impressed him. Years of anger, regret, drugs and prison might have completely screwed him up.

Alex Ortiz junior could be the killer. Some of what Taggart said fit, and some could apply to a lot of people who didn't kill thirteen individuals. Ortiz had a history of rage and drug abuse, and the Councilman's efforts to protect his son had turned a man in his mid-twenties into a spoiled and entitled child who had too much to prove. This potential lead was a keg of dynamite that could blow up Joe's career. He could envision the conversation with Ochoa's father.

"Hi, Councilman Ochoa. I'm sorry to have to arrive at your home unannounced, but I need to speak to your son."

"For what reason, Detective?"

"His name came up regarding a police investigation."

"In what capacity?"

"Well, in addition to being a drug addict and sex maniac, we need to question Alex junior in connection with thirteen murders."

"Oh, I didn't realize. Please come in and I'll bring you to his room."

Joe figured that would not be how this scenario would play out. The councilman would instead stonewall any investigation prior to totally squashing it. The detective had a picture of himself heating up pretzels on a street corner.

Chapter 20

When he returned home, Joe received a phone call from Harry Brenner.

"Glad I caught you," said the chief of detectives.

"I just got in. I was about to go in the backyard for a cigarette and then we're gonna have dinner."

"Sorry to interrupt that, but we have a situation."

"What kind of situation, Harry?" *Was someone spotted wearing white after Labor Day?*

Joe was assuming that he didn't mean that another body had been found. Someone on the Task Force would've contacted him by now about that. But that news certainly wouldn't have shocked him. Brenner's people must have been breathing down his neck, so he needed to transfer some of his problem to Joe. Shit always rolls downhill. Joe wished that it would stop amassing at his door.

"I just spoke with Commissioner Fields, and Captain Sterling paid me a visit today, to give me the heads-up that Fields would be contacting me tonight."

"What's going on, Harry?"

"We'd like for you to report to 1PP tomorrow morning before you head out to the Task Force Command Center."

"Why?"

"The commissioner, along with some politicians, want to talk with you. They have some questions and some concerns."

"I don't have time for this crap, Harry. You know what we're up against and every minute counts. This bureaucratic B.S. is a waste. Can't you just get me out of this? You know how to talk to them."

"This wasn't presented to me as an option, Joe. They want you down there tomorrow morning."

Joe was pacing around the room. "I already have a real ball breaker of a day in store, and now this on top of it."

"I'm sorry Joe. You know I'm on your side, but what can I do? This comes from above, as well as some elected officials who are getting some heat."

"I know. I'm not mad at you. I don't mean to shoot the messenger."

"That's okay," Harry said with a chuckle. "I was ready for your reaction. Fields wants me there as well, so I'll see you tomorrow morning."

"Who else can I expect to grace us with their presence?"

"They're keeping me in the dark about that. Besides Fields and Sterling, I would take an educated guess that Lt. Moss would be in attendance, and I think you can count on Mayor Simpson and Councilman Ortiz being there as well."

"Ortiz?"

"I would assume. He presides over the neighborhoods where many of the bodies were discovered. Is that an issue?"

Joe didn't know whether to share with Harry the details of his breakfast meeting with Clayton Taggart. Joe hadn't told anyone about their conversation.

Earlier that day, the detective found out that Everett Michaels had been sent back to prison shortly after he'd disclosed to Clayton Taggart that Alex Ortiz junior was the serial killer. Joe called an old friend, who was a corrections officer at the prison where Michaels and Taggart had done time together. He shared with Joe that Michaels had been beaten to death the prior week in the laundry room with a mop handle. Apparently, Taggart hadn't been advised of this development. Unless he knew and kept it to himself.

"Do you know who killed Michaels?" Joe asked the corrections officer.

"No, of course nobody saw a thing. Besides, some of the

guards are so freakin' intimidated by these cons."

"What kind of prisoner was he?"

"Nothing really stood out. He wasn't a violent guy. He was in for drug offenses. Why?"

"Did you ever talk to him. Did he ever get any visitors?" asked Joe.

"We spoke a few times. I don't know anything about him getting any visitors. No, wait a minute." There was a long pause.

"What is it?"

"I remember now," his friend said. "Some political guy's kid came to visit Michaels. I thought it was weird at the time because Michaels was an everyday schnook. I didn't figure he had any juice. But a C.O. told me that they had gone to school together, and even been arrested together one time. This political kid was a big-time druggie and scumbag."

"Please, try and remember, could it have been councilman Alex Ortiz's son, Alex Ortiz junior?"

"Yeah, Ortiz, that sounds right. I think it was Ortiz's kid."

"Thanks, you've been a lot of help. I'll be in touch."

"Okay, Joe, glad to help. Talk soon."

Joe put his cell phone back in his pocket and closed his eyes to process this information. Everett Michaels had told Clayton Taggart that Alex Ortix junior was the killer. Taggart shared this with Joe, and now Michaels was dead. Joe wondered if either Taggart or Ortiz's son was aware of that. The detective would have to make a few calls checking into the past relationship between Michaels and Ortiz junior.

He decided to keep Brenner out of the loop for now and addressed his boss's inquiry about Ortiz.

"The councilman and I don't always see eye to eye. It's no big deal. I'm tired and cranky tonight. I'll see you tomorrow."

"Have a good night, Joe."

"You too."

As soon as he hung up, Patty came down the stairs to see who was on the phone.

"It was Brenner. They want me to be at 1 PP at eight tomorrow morning for a meeting."

"Oh," responded Patty, without enthusiasm. She knew that Joe being summoned there was tantamount to a 4th grader being summoned to the principal's office. He wasn't going to get a pat on the back that was for sure. "You want me to start dinner?"

"Yes, thanks. I'm just going up to change and to call Al."

"Tell him I said hello and that he should come over for dinner soon."

"Will do," Joe assured her as he walked upstairs, his suit jacket folded over his right arm, his briefcase in his left hand.

"Hi ya Joey," an enthusiastic Al bellowed into the phone. "Long time no speak. Since Christmas. I figured you boys were up to your neck in it."

"We're up against it, Al, that's for sure. Thirteen bodies that we know about. The Task Force has been operating for three months and we're honestly not much further along than when we started. So few clues and so many dead ends."

"I hear you, and I feel for you guys. Just like me with that Robinson case. We never solved it and I can't get past it. I'll take it to my grave. I pray for a different fate for you and your team. Every night I pray that you catch this maniac."

"Thanks, Al. I just got a call from Brenner. Per the commish, I'm to report to 1 PP at eight tomorrow for some shoe squeezing."

"I'm not surprised. Actually, I thought I may hear from you tonight."

"Are you doing mind reading work in your retirement?"

Al laughed. "No, nothing like that. It is just a piece of news that I read on the Internet, on Yahoo."

Now it was Joe's turn to laugh. "Al, a few years ago you thought the Internet was a kind of device to catch fish and Yahoo was a chocolate flavored drink."

"What can I say, the grandkids are making every effort to modernize me, to take me out of the dark ages when people actually spoke to each other."

"Well, they're succeeding. But what news did you read?"

"Oh, yeah, sorry. I thought you might've heard. I saw an online news item suggesting that the serial killer could be a cop or a former cop. Apparently, some anonymous source from your investigation team said some believe that the perp is a member of the law enforcement community, or a former member."

Joe wasn't aware of this story. He had heard some internal scuttlebutt about this possibility but didn't expect it to be in print. Joe had been chasing the story Taggart had told him all day, started home around six and hadn't turned the radio on in the car. But this explained the sudden need for the brass and the politicians to meet and 'talk' with Joe.

"This is the first I'm hearing of this story, Al. Thanks. At least now I know what to expect tomorrow."

"You can expect a shit storm, my friend, and you don't need me to tell you that. I have the TV news on mute, but I can see that they're discussing this new angle. I'd better let you go."

"Yeah, thanks, buddy. Let me eat, then scan the Internet and the TV news."

"Try to get some sleep too. Tomorrow will be a marathon. I wish you God's speed. Have a good night."

"Thanks. I'll try. Oh, I almost forgot. Patty wanted me to invite you over for dinner soon."

"Sure, love to, when things settle down for you. Be well."

"You too. Thanks again, Al. Talk soon."

With that Joe hung up, changed his clothes and headed downstairs for dinner. He had made a conscious decision not to tell Al about his talk with Clayton Taggart, though he wasn't sure why. Joe knew that he had a long night ahead and even longer day tomorrow. He wondered when this nightmare would be over for him, the city and the families. He didn't have a good feeling that it would be anytime soon and wondered if he could still purchase stock in Gary Carpenter's uranium field in Brooklyn.

Chapter 21

Joe's drive into Manhattan on this January morning was reminiscent of the one he'd taken over three months ago in October. That was the day when he first heard about the decision to name him lead investigator of the newly formed Joint Task Force.

On that day he was lauded for his excellent investigative skills and ability to lead men. They explained to him why he was the right man to head-up the group that would capture the serial killer.

Today the message most likely would be different. Today they'd require answers to their questions and concerns. Joe would be their target today and have to explain why the murderer was still at large.

Joe entered the familiar room at 1PP a few minutes before eight. FBI Agent Russell Hollander was already there drinking his Starbucks coffee. The two had seen each other quite a bit over the last three months and were building a kinship. In the middle of their conversation, Joe noticed that Commissioner Fields, Brenner, Captain Sterling and Lt. Moss had entered the room.

There were some chairs and tables set up. Fields, Hollander and Devlin remained standing at the front of the room. Fields exchanged pleasantries and polite small talk, advising that he'd hold off on beginning the meeting as they were waiting on some more people to attend. Joe wondered if the Spanish Inquisitor Torquemada was one.

After a few minutes, a small group entered the room lead by New York City Mayor Louise Simpson, followed by Queens Borough President Walt Buckner and Councilman

Alex Ortiz. What a lineup, especially with Ortiz taking a seat close to Joe. He reached for a Tums in his inside jacket pocket and popped it into his mouth.

"Now that everyone is here," Commissioner Fields said, "we can get started. I'm going to ask FBI Agent Hollander and Det. Devlin to stay up front with me."

Joe would rather have been seated. It would have been more difficult for the firing squad to hit him.

Fields said, "I called this meeting because I felt it necessary on many levels. I wanted all interested parties to be in the same room at the same time to avoid miscommunication, and so we can address mutual concerns."

Fields took a sip of water from a Poland Spring bottle that sat on a table to his right. "I need to address a concern of mine. We've all heard the rumors about a task force member leaking a story to the press that a current or former member of the law enforcement community was a target of our investigation. This is erroneous and completely without merit. We've contacted media outlets to have this false information retracted, but as you know the media has felt stonewalled by us."

Everyone present knew the elephant in the room; the idea that the 'Period Killer' could be an individual who presently, or formerly, carried a badge. Devlin gave Fields credit for addressing the elephant and taking some blame for it. "Now, I've spoken to Russell Hollander and Harry Brenner and both assured me that they have absolutely no knowledge of the genesis of this alleged source, or if such a source actually exists."

"Further, Detective Devlin, upon returning to the Command Center will begin an inquiry into this matter. I have his assurance that the accusation is totally baseless."

Joe tugged at his shirt collar and forced a smile. He tried in earnest to hide his surprise. Both declarations uttered by Fields were news to him. He hadn't spoken at all to the commissioner, or anyone else, regarding this breaking development, and had heard about it from Al only eleven hours ago. The idea that they could be looking for an individual with a law enforcement background was plausible. This killer clearly had knowledge of law enforcement techniques which have allowed him to avoid detection.

Fields then motioned toward Devlin. "This is Detective Joe Devlin. I don't wish to speak for him or put words in his mouth, which is why I 've called him here today to address your concerns."

Joe stood, rubbing his hands together. "Good morning. Thank you, Commissioner Fields. I want to begin by reiterating the thoughts of the commissioner in that I have absolutely no knowledge of any individual within my team who has leaked information to the media. In addition, our team is not following any lead regarding the idea that our guy has any connection to the criminal justice system."

Joe saw Mayor Louise Simpson shift in her chair, crossing her right leg over her left. She said, "We appreciate your diligence, Detective." The mayor had smooth ebony skin and midnight black hair. As she spoke, she tucked a lock of hair behind her ear.

"Thank you, Madam Mayor."

"Please, don't read me wrong, Detective. The mayor's office is second to none in admiration for the hard work done by the NYPD, especially under these extremely trying circumstances. But we must be responsive to our constituents, all of whom would like to know what's being done. We're very concerned about these thirteen unsolved murders in our city, and disappointed that your Task Force has been operating with little to no progress."

"I'm sensitive to your situation just as hopefully you are sensitive to our plight," Joe said. "Our team has been receiving numerous leads. Unfortunately, we haven't found any serious suspects. We've questioned and interrogated some, but there wasn't enough credible evidence to hold any of them. I can assure that we are working tirelessly on this."

Joe calculated that this might not be the best time to bring up the fact that a former C.I. had fingered Alex Ortiz junior as the killer.

"That's all well and good," Councilman Alex Ortiz said, "but as you are aware, Detective, the city is on the verge of panic. The citizens in the communities being targeted, such as my district, feel helpless and need to know what steps are being taken. I held a town hall meeting last night, attended by both Mayor Simpson and Queens Borough President Buckner, to address the fears of my constituents."

Joe was thankful that he'd been left off the guest list.

The councilman plucked at the cuff of his shirt. "It's our contention that the police aren't being responsive to our needs and concerns. Now, we hear a news report that the serial killer could be an individual with a connection to the NYPD. My community needs more assurances that all that can be done is being done, and we require more frequent communication."

Joe wanted to ask the councilman if he knew his son's whereabouts on the nights of the murders. He also would've loved to question him about Alex junior's relationship with the now deceased Everett Michaels. The detective resisted the urge.

Mayor Simpson said, "Please don't misunderstand. We don't believe that police personnel are involved. But I was in attendance last night at Councilman Ortiz's Town Hall meeting, and those who voiced their apprehension were of the same opinion that he just shared. They feel like there are too many snags and delays."

"I understand how you feel, Madam Mayor," Joe said. "We have a room at the Command Center dedicated to those who were killed by this serial killer. Not just names, but individuals with families and friends. We never lose sight of that and we'll keep that room until we have our man in custody.

"We understand how important the role of the media is

and I apologize if we've been remiss in not sharing information. Believe me, we're not stonewalling. We follow up all credible leads, and wherever the investigation takes us is where it takes us.

"Let me conclude by saying that we'll do a better job of sharing legitimate information, and that I'll try to determine who this unidentified individual is, or if the story is a total fabrication, which I believe it is."

Commissioner Fields thanked Joe for his words and efforts. Those assembled shook hands and wished each other luck. The brass congratulated Joe reminded him that the politicians had made their voices heard, and that they'd not relent until the killer was caught. Joe shook his head knowingly, said his good-byes and headed to his precinct. Maybe something had broken while he was at headquarters. There was a better chance that it hadn't.

Chapter 22

Joe staggered through his front door around 8:00 p.m. the same night. He dropped his briefcase and suit jacket on the couch and headed straight for his pal, Johnnie Walker. He showered his favorite brand of Scotch with a few ice cubes. Joe stirred with his index finger and slumped into his recliner. The remote was sitting on an end-table out of his reach, and he was in no mood to chase it. Instead, he decided to nurse his frustration, along with his drink.

The house was silent. Joe couldn't remember the last time that Patty wasn't home when he finished his day. Prior to the death of their son, Patty worked in an insurance office and was active in various groups and charities. Since that time, she hadn't returned to work and slowly pulled away from social interactions. Joe felt increasingly helpless as Patty became more and more depressed.

His wife's first psychiatrist had prescribed Zoloft to combat her social-anxiety and post-traumatic stress disorder. When she didn't feel better, Patty sought out another psychiatrist, who switched her to Lexapro to fight depression. Finally, she gave up on doctors and their miracle drugs. "There's no cure for life," she told Joe.

Some days the detective could barely keep it together. Eight years later, Thomas' death had affected the two differently. Patty's sadness was intensifying while Joe's anger grew. He sipped his whiskey and closed his eyes in his recliner.

About fifteen minutes later Patty arrived, startling Joe as she entered their home. A groggy Devlin asked, "Hi, where've you been?"

"At my sister's house. Sorry, I lost track of time. I ate dinner with Elizabeth. Do you want me to make you something?"

"No, I ate a late lunch and am exhausted. I'm glad you got out of the house today."

"Me too. I don't blame you feeling so tired. You were up so early for your trip to Manhattan. You must be bushed"

"I am. I'm going to stay down here for a while then come up to bed."

"Did your day go well?"

"Let me put it this way, on my way home I stepped in a pile of dog crap, and that was the highlight. I left my shoes out on the porch."

Patty's mouth curved into a smile. "I saw them out there. I chose not to inquire. Oh, I almost forgot. Sam wants you to call him."

Normally in the midst of a backbreaking investigation Joe would put this request on the back burner. But for Elizabeth and Samuel Weiss, he would move it to the front burner. In the brutal aftermath of Thomas' death, they'd always been there for the Devlins. "Whatever you want, whatever you need, anytime and anyplace." That was the Weiss' mantra. Aunt Elizabeth and Uncle Samuel had doted on Thomas, as he was their only nephew and they didn't have children of their own. His death was a crushing blow to them as well. Joe placed his glass onto a coaster and pulled himself from his recliner.

"What's up?" Joe asked.

"She didn't say."

"Okay, I'll give him a call."

"Thank you, Joe, but try not to be too long. I know when you guys talk it can take all night. You need to get some rest."

"No problem. I'll just see what he needs. Be up soon."

"Sounds good," said Patty as she made her way upstairs.

Samuel answered his cell phone on the second ring. "Joe,

thanks for calling."

"Sure thing. Heard through the grapevine you wanted to speak with me."

"Yes, I do. I must confess I'm a little embarrassed to ask this of you, given your position in the NYPD. And if you can't help, I'll completely understand. It's just that, well, you know, sometimes these types of things make me anxious."

Joe didn't have the slightest ideas what Sam was referring to.

"How can I help you? What can I do?"

"I don't want to make a federal case out of this. But I got a speeding ticket a few weeks ago, not from a cop but from one of those Traffic Enforcement Cameras. I just got the ticket in the mail today. It's my first time ever having any interaction with the police in my life, for anything. I've never even gotten a parking ticket."

Joe believed that. Samuel was not exactly known in his circle as the adventurous type. His idea of wild was to use blue ink for accounts payable instead of black.

"If there was some way you could help me. I know it seems silly. It's not the money. I will still pay the fine. I hate to impose or overreach, but is there something you could do?"

How could Joe say no to Sam? He owed him this favor plus more than he could count. Joe responded in the only way appropriate.

"I'm sorry, Sam, but our entire conversation was recorded and has been transmitted to FBI Headquarters in Quantico, Virginia. It's likely that they have dispatched a unit to your home as we speak. When they arrive, make no statement. Wait for your attorney. You will then be taken into custody and brought in for questioning. Please say your good-byes to Elizabeth now."

There was dead silence on the other end of the phone. Joe heard what sounded like faint gasps for air. He loved to tease Sam, who was a tremendous guy, but had little sense of humor.

"Sam, are you still with me?" Joe asked chuckling. He could hear the relief through their cell phone connection.

"Oh, you bastard. I'm just now catching my breath. I had visions of wearing an orange jumpsuit and eating oatmeal that tastes like gravel. I can't believe I fell for that line of bull. I must remember this when I do your taxes."

"Tell me about the ticket."

"A couple of weeks ago a few colleagues and I went to dinner on Van Doren Street in the Corona section of Queens."

Joe knew the area very well. He'd walked a beat there in his early days on the force. Corona was in the north-central portion of Queens, and, ironically, was also part of Councilman Alex Ortiz's district.

"On my way home, one of those Traffic Enforcement Cameras photographed me going 51 in a 35 mile per hour zone. I swear, Joe, I had no alcohol at dinner, and I had no idea I was travelling at that speed."

"I believe you, but you need to relax. It's not like you sold secrets to the Russians."

"You're right, I'm blowing this whole thing out of proportion. But I'm a law-abiding citizen. You know that."

"I promise you, it's no big thing. Some of these freakin' politicians should be so lucky as to have a speeding ticket be their worst indiscretion. I'll take care of this. Could you tell me on what date you got the ticket and at what time?"

"Oh, sure. It was on January 14th at 10:37 p.m. Thank you for your help, Joe. But if this is something that will cause you grief or potential backlash, please pretend that this matter was never discussed."

"Put this thing out of your mind. It won't be an issue. For you, it's my pleasure."

"Well, okay then, as long as your career will not be adversely affected."

Devlin had neither the time nor the strength to explain to

Weiss how little his career meant to him currently. At one point, it meant almost everything. Since his son's death, it meant less and less each day. Joe wondered at what point he would walk away and go sit on a beach, or in a pool hall.

"Consider this a down payment on what I owe you. It'll cause me no issues in the department. Remember, I'm a detective, one of the good guys."

"We're family, Joe. You owe me nothing. I appreciate this gesture very much. I was so embarrassed that I never even told Elizabeth. Please don't tell Patty."

"Are you afraid that they'll revoke your parking spot at the Larchmont Rotary Club?"

"Always with the jokes."

"Seriously, I'll handle it. Pretend like it never happened."

"If you say so. Thanks again. But there is a fine of $80.00. How do I pay that?"

"Make a donation to your favorite charity. Maybe the Police Athletic League."

"Good thinking. I'll do so, and I'll sweeten the amount a little. Thanks again."

After they said their goodbyes and vowed to get together soon, Joe hung up the phone, slumped back in his recliner and went back to sipping his cocktail. First thing tomorrow he would keep his promise to Sam. After finishing his drink, he made his way upstairs.

Patty had just tucked herself into bed when Joe entered the room. Her neatly combed brunette hair bounced against her shoulders as she moved to turn on her lamp. His wife's fragile cocoa brown eyes stared at him.

"I was just going to read for a while. You look exhausted. I assume you aren't going for a walk tonight?" she said.

Joe barely had the energy to collapse. "No, not tonight."

"Good. You've hardly been sleeping. Please try to get some rest tonight."

"I will. Just need a few minutes then I'm turning in."

"Oh, I forgot to ask, what did Sam want?"

Joe remembered that Sam had asked him not to let Patty know.

"He asked if I'd go with him to see the St. John's game at Madison Square Garden on Saturday. I told him that under normal circumstances I'd love to go, but with the Task Force I wouldn't be able to make it. He understood."

Patty shook her head. "That's too bad. I know how you love basketball, and you could use a night out. Are you sure you can't make it?"

"I really can't. I need to be available this weekend."

"I understand. I admire your dedication. I'm sure he understood."

"He always does."

Chapter 23

Joe woke up around 5:30 a.m. He no longer needed an alarm. The heat from the brass was beginning to singe his socks, and his mind and body tossed all night.

As Joe slid out of bed, Patty woke up.

With one eye open, she asked him, "What are you doing up so early? Are you going into Manhattan again?"

"No, babe. Just getting an early start. Go back to sleep."

He couldn't tell Patty about the favor his brother-in-law had asked of him. Before Joe headed out to his precinct and a meeting with Brenner, who would greet him with a long face, a short temper and rapid-fire questions, he'd have to make a stop at the Queens Traffic Violations Bureau.

Joe merged onto the Long Island Expressway on route to the QTVB in Flushing. He still had some pals there, pals who wouldn't break his shoes about his business there, pals who wouldn't be asking questions.

Joe entered the building a few minutes past 8:00 a.m. His badge, along with his prior relationship with an officer, got him past security. Last night's phone call to Stan Marsh, a former drinking acquaintance and QTVB big wig, directed Joe to the location where he needed to go to conduct his business.

Upon arriving on the lower level, he was greeted by Officer Diane Mooney. Her blonde hair was pinned neatly beneath her NYPD uniform cap. She had fiery blue eyes.

"Good morning, may I help you?" a surprisingly cheerful Officer Mooney inquired. It was 8:10 a.m. and this building's personnel didn't exactly have the reputation of being full of Saturday Night Live skit writers.

Joe flashed his badge, which Diane glanced at. "Hello, I'm Detective Joe Devlin. I believe you're expecting me."

"I am, Detective. Supervisor Marsh informed me you'd be arriving this morning. I understand you two go way back."

"Yes, we do. Maybe we can be friends anyway."

Officer Mooney laughed. "I heard from the guys here that you two have a good relationship. Supervisor Marsh has always been courteous and pleasant in our rare interactions."

"Good, but if you had constant interactions your opinion may differ. Anyway, did he explain my business here?"

"No, he didn't have to. He asked me to accommodate you in any way possible. What can I help you with?"

"I just need to use one of your computers to look into a ticket issued by one of the Speed Cameras, given to a potential suspect in our investigation of the serial killer."

She nodded. "Happy to help in any way possible."

"That's very kind of you Officer, but all I need is access to a computer. Stan said that you could provide me with sign-on information. I'd be very appreciative."

"Certainly, right this way, Detective." Officer Mooney ushered Joe to a series of computer screens set atop a long, laminated desk in the far corner of the room.

"Thank you so much. I'll let you know when my work is completed."

"Take your time. We don't move at a rapid pace down here."

Joe sat at the appropriate computer and began to scroll through hundreds of drivers who were issued tickets. *Who knew this many individuals were getting caught by these cameras?* No wonder New York City installed them, Joe thought. They were moneymakers.

Upon observing the surfeit of tickets issued just on the day he was looking for, he figured out how to narrow his search, checking now only for speeding tickets issued on Van Doren Street in Corona after 10:30 p.m. Devlin was going frame by frame until he hoped he'd see the familiar black BMW driven by Sam Weiss. Per Marsh's information regarding the location of cameras in that area, Joe knew that Weiss had gotten the ticket on Van Doren Street just before its intersection with the Horace Harding Expressway.

Finally, there it was in full color on his computer screen. A picture of Sam Weiss' vehicle, including front and back plates, and a picture of Weiss. Marsh had explained to Joe last night that new technology enabled these cameras to photograph the vehicle, the plates and the driver. In addition, Marsh instructed him on the proper way to eradicate a ticket. Joe's tech friends had explained that things don't ever really get fully expunged, but Marsh's method would make detection of this ticket virtually impossible.

Further, the vehicle wasn't involved in an accident or crime, so Joe figured they were in the clear. He followed Marsh's instructions and soon had accomplished his task. Joe scrolled back a few vehicles, then forward, satisfied that the ticket issued to Weiss no longer was there.

As Joe's mind was cluttered and jumbled with thoughts of Sam, speeding tickets and serial killers, he scrolled ahead on the computer past 10:37 p.m. to see a few more drivers who had been caught in the trap of the Eye in the Sky. Joe mindlessly wound forward, half-noticing the vehicles and their occupants, until something caught his eye and made him look at the screen more closely. At 10:43 p.m., a gray Honda Accord had received a speeding ticket at the same location that his brother-in-law had gotten one. The car was unfamiliar to Joe, but the driver he recognized. It was his neighbor, Jim Bradley. An incredible coincidence, Joe thought. He realized that Bradley wasn't driving his own vehicle, which was a Mercedes SUV. This wasn't a federal crime. However, it seemed strange that Bradley would be driving this sedan instead of his own SUV in Queens on a weeknight close to 11:00 p.m. Joe leaned back in his chair, interlocked his hands behind his head, stared at the ceiling and then slowly closed his eyes. This was a favorite thinking position for him, but one thing was missing. His eyes shot open, he swiveled his chair around and bellowed for Officer Mooney.

"Yes, Joe, what is it?"

"Do you mind if I smoke?"

"It's ok with me. I'm the only one here until 9:00 a.m., and when the guys come in they don't exactly hit the ground running."

"Marsh told me that, off the record. I gather the 9:00 a.m. crew gulps coffee, inhales donuts, does crossword puzzles and takes turns in the lavatory."

"Off the record, even that is giving them too much credit."

"Thanks. Just one quick cigarette and then I'm gone."

"Take your time."

Joe lit up, took a long drag, exhaled through his mouth and nostrils, and returned to thinking about his neighbor. The video was not damning in and of itself, but he'd been a detective for a long time and had a sixth sense about certain things. He followed his nose and his ulcer. Both were useful in crime detection.

Joe also possessed a terrific memory. It had betrayed him a little the last few years, but it still was a valuable asset. With eyes closed and cigarette burning between his index and middle fingers, he pondered this newest development. Something was bothering him, but he couldn't put his finger on it. Suddenly, he sprang forward in his chair. A recollection just come back to him in a flash. He took a quick drag of his Marlboro and then crushed it out in a makeshift ashtray. A pad and pens were resting in a bin in the upper right-hand corner of the desk. Joe wanted to jot down some notes so he wouldn't forget. Having a great memory was one thing, but trusting it was another, and Joe wanted to ensure that this information was recorded.

What he remembered was that on the night of January 14th he'd seen Jim Bradley. They'd been taking their garbage cans to the curb at the same time. It was the same night of the basketball game between the New York Knicks and Boston Celtics. Both men had laughed at the fact that they'd chosen to pull their garbage cans to the street during halftime. The game had started a little after 7:00 p.m., and the halftime began sometime around 8:15. That meant that he'd seen James Bradley around 8:20 p.m. at the foot of his driveway. Bradley subsequently received a speeding ticket from a camera approximately two hours and twenty minutes later in Queens, in a car that wasn't his.

"A little strange," Joe thought. He wrote down all of the relevant information regarding the ticket his neighbor had received, including the license plate number of the gray Honda that was being operated at the time. Upon returning to his precinct, he'd run the plate number to see to whom the car belonged.

This could be a lead, or it could be nothing more than a strange coincidence. Since the trail was not hot, or warm, or even tepid, Joe felt there was no harm in pursuing this inquiry and seeing where it went.

Devlin gathered his belongings, shut down the computer and made his way back to the front of the room where Officer Mooney was working.

"I want to thank you for your courtesy," he said.

"It was my pleasure. I trust your visit here had a successful ending."

"It did. If Marsh actually shows up to work, please thank him and tell him I got the information I needed."

"He rarely comes to the lower level, but when I see him, I'll share your message."

"He'll probably still have his bowling shoes on."

"I plead the Fifth," she said.

Joe returned to his car with his mind awash in questions. He'd arrived at the QVTB with three suspects, and now had added a person of interest. Only three he could question due to the recent demise of Everett Michaels in prison.

It had been two days since his breakfast meeting with

Clayton Taggart. He'd been unable to reach his former C.I. since. Joe called his cell phone numerous times and left messages with no response. The detective hoped that Taggart had not met the same fate as Michaels.

A conversation with councilman Ortiz's son was on the agenda. He also wanted to dig into the past relationship between Ortiz and Michaels. The meeting at 1PP and the call from Sam Weiss had sidetracked Joe. He had to tread lightly in this area. Questioning a politician's son regarding serial murders had to be done with some finesse, which was not always Joe's strength.

The detective considered his neighbor Jim Bradley. A man whose family had opened up their home to Patty and him on Thanksgiving. A man still grieving deeply over the loss of his brother. *How could he be mixed up in this?* It didn't make any sense. But a feeling kept gnawing at him. Whenever he ignored such feelings, he regretted it. Joe knew interrogating Ortiz could be a career killer, but questioning a friend, especially one who had suffered so much, was not an easy task either.

On the way back to his precinct, the detective saw a billboard advertising a trip to sunny San Diego. Someday, he thought. Joe wished it could be today.

Chapter 24

Joe had hoped to return to his precinct around 9:00 a.m. However, his discovery of Jim Bradley on camera delayed his departure from the QTVB. As he parked, he had a feeling he'd be greeted by Brenner who wouldn't be wearing a party hat.

It was almost 9:30 a.m. as Joe closed his car door, stamped out his cigarette and made his way toward the building. He needed a few minutes to have coffee and get organized at his desk.

Joe entered the building as a teenager would enter his home after curfew. His head was down, hoping to duck any notice. Brenner was already there, to greet Devlin as an angry father would.

"Nice of you to join us, Joe. We certainly hope that we didn't drag you away from anything important."

It was unlike Brenner to be so snarky. The higher-ups must have had his buns for breakfast, and he was here to add Devlin to the buffet line.

"Sorry, Harry, it couldn't be helped," Joe said.

"Alright, let's get to work." Brenner ushered Joe toward the Command Center. Captain Sterling was not present, yet FBI Criminal Profiler Russell Hollander was.

"Good morning, Russell, nice to see you again," Joe said.

"Nice to be back. Sorry I haven't been around much since the holidays. They had me assigned to another case in Chicago that we just closed. I understand we aren't much farther along than when I left. Brenner briefed me about the progress made since my absence."

"We're not happy with the status of the investigation,"

Brenner said.

"Let me take a look at what you have. We should bring all the members of the Task Force in and make a plan. I hate to say we're essentially starting from scratch, but we're essentially starting from scratch."

"Okay," Joe said. "I'll get the team together and we'll see where we are and what the next step should be."

"Okay, men, I'll leave you to it" Brenner said. "Just keep me updated so I can advise the commissioner and the captain of any developments. Also, let me know of any resources you might require."

Hollander and Devlin thanked Brenner and assured him that they'd keep him in the loop.

With that Brenner exited the 115, and Devlin and Hollander began to round up the team.

Joe told Russell he needed a few minutes to follow up on a lead from earlier that morning. He assured Russell he'd only need a few minutes and then he'd meet up with the team and press forward. Russell nodded in agreement, took a note handed to him and walked toward his desk.

Joe made his way outside of the Command Center to his regular desk. He picked up the phone, but then decided against making a call. At this point, he wasn't sure if he wanted anyone to hear his conversation, or even be apprised of a possible new development. Joe wasn't sure why he felt this way, but was certain that, for now, he would keep any information to himself. Eventually he would share what he hoped to learn. Perhaps. Maybe.

Joe took out the pad that contained the plate number for the car he had seen Jim Bradley driving at the time he was issued a speeding ticket in Queens. A plate search revealed that the vehicle in question was registered to a Michelle Wagner, who resided in Nassau County. The name didn't ring a bell to Devlin. He racked his brain but couldn't place it, but he felt that it was familiar.

Because most of the personnel in the precinct was either

tied up with the serial killer investigation or any one of a dozen other homicides, nobody was paying attention to what Joe was doing. That being the case, he proceeded on with his interest in Ms. Wagner.

Through some digging and a call to an old colleague, Joe learned a few details about the woman in question, one being that she worked an overnight shift as a nurse at New York County Hospital. Joe smiled, as now he could place her. She was the sister-in-law of Jim Bradley, whom he'd met at his neighbor's house on Thanksgiving. He recalled that she'd been married to Bradley's brother.

Joe wasn't what to make of this information. It was no surprise that Jim might remain close to his widowed sister-in-law, even to the point where he might borrow her car on occasion. But he *was* surprised to discover him driving her car around 10:40 p.m. on the same night that the two men had exchanged thoughts about the Knicks game a few hours earlier.

Joe tried to remember if he'd seen Bradley's SUV sitting in his driveway on the evening in question. While he couldn't swear to it, he was fairly certain that he had. Not positive, but confident. If the SUV was there, why did Bradley need to borrow his sister-in-law's car? One explanation was that the SUV was not operational, but Joe thought he recalled Bradley pulling it out of his driveway the following morning on his way to the train station. Again, he wasn't certain, but fairly sure.

Joe sat back in his chair, running his hands through his hair. He needed a smoke. What he really needed was a drink, but that might not look good in front of the precinct, so he settled for a cigarette. He went outside, lit up and pondered this new information.

What did these details add up to? If Joe started with the premise that Bradley's SUV had been in his driveway that night, and the same vehicle had been driven the following morning, he had to be suspicious of the fact that Bradley needed to borrow Ms. Wagner's car.

Joe rocked back and forth. He shivered slightly as he puffed away on this cold late January morning. What he was considering also made him shiver. There were so many questions that he didn't know where to begin. Even if he let his mind wander to the idea that his neighbor was in Queens on that night for sinister purposes, he had little to nothing to go on. However, Joe felt that he should follow his nose and see where it took him.

Joe flicked his cigarette to the ground and watched it roll down a sewer grate. He knew that he should return to the Command Center and brief them on this information. His head suggested it, but his heart rejected it. Maybe after he followed this lead for a while and developed more concrete evidence, he would bring this to them. Maybe not.

Checking his watch, he knew he had to report back inside and see what Hollander and the team were up to. Most likely spinning their wheels. In addition to the fact that he'd spent more time than he thought he would outside, he also wanted to retrieve his notes and other details he'd gathered regarding this new information and put it in his briefcase for safekeeping. Not to hide it, but rather to keep it confidential until the appropriate time.

The ringing of his cell phone interrupted Joe's thoughts. A voice on the other end advised Joe that his former C.I., Clayton Taggart, had been found dead in his apartment of an apparent drug overdose. It could be an apparent suicide, Joe thought. Or an apparent homicide.

He was not shocked to hear this news. Taggart had not returned any of Joe's calls. Within the last day or so, both Everett Michaels and Clayton Taggart had been found dead. If either were the killer, their secret likely had died with them.

Joe's next move would be to question Alex Ortiz junior. If the councilman's son was involved in the murders, he had a strong motive to silence both men. The detective had to be cautious in this matter, but he couldn't put it off any longer.

Both Alex Ortiz Junior and Jim Bradley were now on Joe's radar. Interrogating these suspects would present difficult, and entirely different, challenges.

Joe slowly walked inside, wondering why he hadn't taken over his dad's plumbing business.

Chapter 25

Joe parked his car in front of Councilman Alex Ortiz's Queens split-level home. As he was pulling the key from the ignition, Brenner shifted uncomfortably in the passenger seat, his eyes on Joe.

"Hold on for a minute. Remember, we can't go in there with guns blazing. The commissioner arranged this meeting, and I promised him we'd deal with them professionally. Yes, there are questions we need answers to, but we were instructed not to take an accusatorial tone or Ortiz will shut us down. Their lawyer won't be present, and we don't want to go down that road."

"I know Harry, I understand. I spoke to the commissioner and assured him that this would be more of an informal thing, not an interrogation. I don't need them lawyering up. If this bears fruit, we'll need to discuss our next step."

"Good. As long as we are on the same page. Let's go."

Last night Joe had phoned Harry to fill him in on the details surrounding the newly deceased Everett Michaels and Clayton Taggart, as well as Alex Ortiz junior. Harry told him he would speak to the commissioner. Fields then contacted the councilman who acquiesced to the meeting. Joe wasn't certain what the commissioner relayed to his colleague, but he knew they had a decent relationship. Besides, an elected official could not be perceived as stonewalling an investigation, especially one this high profile.

Harry rang the bell and Councilman Ortiz, wearing a light blue shirt, tan pants and a dark blue sport jacket answered the door. He had a chiseled face and thick, dark hair. "Good morning, detectives, please come in."

"Thank you for agreeing to see us," Harry said.

"It is nice to see you both again. Please sit down."

As soon as the detectives sat on the couch, Alex Ortiz junior came down the stairs to join them. He said hello and fell into a recliner. The councilman sat on a smaller couch with a placid expression. Junior looked like the previous night had been a rough one. His hair was mussed and his eyes bloodshot. He was wearing wrinkled gray sweatpants and a St. John's University red hoodie. Nobody else seemed to be home.

The councilman began. "So, Commissioner Fields explained that you needed to speak to me regarding your investigation."

"Well, we really need to speak to your son," Harry said.

"Yes, Ted mentioned that as well. How can we help you?"

Joe leaned forward. "We're hoping that Alex could answer a few questions. This won't take long."

"What do you want?" Alex asked, his eyes struggling to stay open.

"Do you know an Everett Michaels?" Joe asked.

"Sure. We went to high school together. We've lost touch the last few years, though. His life went in a different direction than mine. You know, drugs, that kinda thing."

"And in what direction has your life gone?"

"What do you mean?"

"I mean, well, what do you do for a living?"

"I help out my dad with fundraising and campaigning."

"When was the last time you saw Mr. Michaels?"

"Maybe a few months back. I can't really remember. I do remember that it was a pretty wild night."

"Yes, I heard," Joe said, smirking.

"What do you mean you heard, heard from who?" Alex said in a raised voice, pushing himself out of the recliner.

"Did you know that Mr. Michaels was killed in prison?" Joe asked.

Ortiz Jr.'s face paled. "Everett's dead? No, I wasn't aware

of that. But what's that got to do with me? And who the hell's running his mouth?"

"A former C.I. of mine named Clayton Taggart. He just died of an apparent drug overdose. Did you know him?"

"I'm getting uncomfortable with the tenor of this conversation," Councilman Ortiz said gruffly. "Gentlemen, just what are you trying to imply?"

Harry shot Joe a look that said, *'Don't push this!'*

"I'm sorry if we got off track here," Joe said. "We think that Mr. Michaels may have known something about the murders, maybe crossed paths with someone we need to question. We were just hoping that your son could give us the names of people who Michaels hung around with or bought drugs from."

Alex's shoulders slumped and he sat back down. "Like I said, we lost touch over the years. I wouldn't know any of those people. I'm out of the drug scene. I used to have a problem, but I'm off the stuff. I'm straight."

Joe felt Alex's look and behavior belied that comment.

"What about Clayton Taggart, did you ever meet him?"

The councilman held his left hand up towards his son. "Again, detective, I don't know where you're going with this. Obviously, we want to cooperate, but my son has not been involved with Everett Michaels in years, and he doesn't know this Mr. Taggart."

"Can't he speak for himself?" Joe asked.

Alex leaned forward in his chair and yelled, "Of course I can speak for myself! I told you. I don't know anything about these guys or any murders."

"We're just gathering information," Harry said, adjusting the lapels of his jacket. "We think these two men may have known something about the deaths, been involved in some way, and were subsequently silenced. Detective Devlin and I are speaking with anyone who had a prior relationship. It's a long shot, but we must check out any possible lead. We know your son and Michaels go back a ways and thought he might be able to give us a few names to pursue. That's the extent of it."

"Well I don't," Alex said. "I told you, I've got a job and am away from all of that."

"I'm sorry we couldn't be of more assistance, detectives," the councilman said.

"Okay, thanks for taking the time," Harry said.

They all rose to shake hands. As they were on their way out, Joe turned to Alex.

"Do you own a gun?"

The councilman's face turned a reddish purple, his fists clenched, and a vein popped out in his neck. "What's this got to do with your investigation? That's none of your god damn business. Your question is completely out of bounds, Detective. We agreed to this without the benefit of my attorney, and you ambush us!"

"I'm just trying to understand the entire picture, councilman."

"I'll fill you in on the picture," yelled the Councilman, pointing his finger at Joe. "You guys have nothing, nothing at all, and you're feeling the pressure and looking for a scapegoat. Yes, my son had some drug issues years ago, end of subject. But he knows absolutely nothing about these horrible murders."

"We didn't mean to get off on the wrong foot here," Harry said.

"Never mind that crap. I'll be on the phone with the commissioner before you're back in your car." He turned to Joe. "Detective, I suggest that you look elsewhere for your killer, and for your career."

"I apologize if I overstepped. I'm trying to do my job. We've got thirteen murders and we never know where our investigation will lead."

"Right now, it's leading out the door. Good-bye."

With that the door slammed behind them.

The detectives stared at each other, then returned to their

vehicle. Joe braced for Harry's reaction.

"Didn't we discuss this, Joe? Didn't we say not to make waves. And you create a tsunami."

"I know Harry, and I'm sorry. But I needed to see their reaction."

"Well, you saw it, and heard it. Loudly."

"I did," Joe said with a wry smile.

"What?"

"The kid has a temper, and the old man has a hell of a temper."

"And?"

"And I wonder if we were questioning the wrong Ortiz!"

Chapter 26

Jim Bradley arrived home and was set upon by Anakin, happily and hungrily waiting at the door. After dropping his briefcase on the couch and removing his coat, he made a B-line to the sliding glass doors. Once outside, his dog tended to his business and Jim tended to their meal.

After eating, Jim was heading upstairs when his doorbell rang. He opened the door to see his neighbor Joe Devlin standing on his porch.

"Good evening, Counselor." Joe's eyes then caught Anakin's gaze. "Hey, how's my pal doing tonight?"

Anakin met Joe's extended hand with his paw, graciously accepted a pat on his head, and went back to his bed for a nap. "That's a terrific dog you have there, Jim."

Jim got a good laugh out of the Joe-Anakin interaction. They seemed to be slowly forming a bond, similar to the way the two men were.

"Good evening, Detective. And thank you. Yes, he's a good boy. Spoiled. But I love him."

Jim and Joe had gotten friendly since their families shared Thanksgiving, but not "show up at my door after work unannounced" friendly, so naturally Jim was curious about the visit. He hoped nothing was wrong with Joe's wife.

"What brings you out on this chilly night?" Jim inquired.

"Well, forgive me for not calling first, but Patty's at her sister's for the night and I thought maybe you'd be up for a walk, or to grab some dinner?"

Jim wondered why his neighbor hadn't called or texted first. They had exchanged cell phone numbers shortly after the holiday. Still, he was grateful for the invitation as eating alone was lonely most nights. The two men did have a passion for walking, and had met up a few times in the neighborhood to stretch their legs. Jim had been to dinner at the Devlins a few times and always had a pleasant evening. Jim sensed that Joe, like himself, had few friends and at times needed a little male companionship.

Having run all this through his mind very quickly Jim figured it wouldn't be such a bad idea to spend a little time with his neighbor.

"Sure, that would be great. I was going to walk a little tonight then go to the Leaning Tower for a few slices. You're welcome to come if you haven't eaten already."

"As a matter of fact, I haven't. Just got home from work. How about we meet at the end of my driveway at 7:30 p.m.?"

"Sounds like a plan. See you then."

"Good, see you in a few."

With that Devlin went home and Jim made his way upstairs, with the sound of Anakin snoring in the background.

They met and began their walk from Forest Avenue to Greene Avenue and were now crossing onto Liberty Blvd.

"Is this the normal route you take?" Jim asked. Or do you mix it up?"

"I keep it fairly routine and basic. You?"

"I'm a creature of habit myself."

"You ever vary the route or the distance?"

"At times," Jim said. "Some nights I'll go a little longer. It depends on the type of day I've had."

"I know what you mean."

As they passed Maury's bagels on Pine Avenue, Joe turned to Jim and said, "Hey, I've been meaning to tell you something. You'll get a kick out of this. Do you remember that night last month, the night of the Knicks-Celtics game when we both put our garbage cans out at the same time? We were bitching about the Knicks."

"Sure, how could I forget. Regrettably, I don't have many

sports conversations anymore. Nothing like two guys complaining about tall millionaires in short pants. What about it?"

"Well," Joe said, "it isn't really a knee slapper. My brother-in-law, Sam, got a ticket that very same night in Queens. One of those New Age-Big Brother Traffic Cameras caught him speeding on Van Doren Street in Corona. That little nebbish. You should've heard him on the phone. You would think they caught him with three prostitutes, two grams of coke and a partridge in a pear tree."

Jim laughed. "I met him when I was at your home for dinner. Nice guy."

"Yes. Very sweet and very loyal. I thought you'd enjoy that. In my early days on the NYPD I walked a beat in that part of Queens. Joe stopped talking as they reached Breyer Street, the home of The Leaning Tower of Pizza."

Vincenzo Napoli, a warm and convivial host, greeted the two men as they came inside. He spoke to them with his old-world charm and with his "it's good for business" accent.

"Good evening, Detective Devlin. Where is the lovely Mrs. Devlin this evening?"

"She's visiting her sister Vin. Mr. Bradley will be my dining companion tonight."

Vincenzo glanced at his pal Jim with a smile. "Well, that's certainly a few steps down."

Jim was used to Vinnie's warm greetings. "Nice to see you tonight, Vin. So, the Board of Health gave you another week."

The three men laughed as Vincenzo showed them to a table and wished them Buon Appetito.

"He's a piece of work," Joe said. "A neighbor recommended this place to Patty and me after we moved in a few years back. The food is excellent. We had an anniversary party here for Patty's sister Elizabeth and her husband, Sam, the speed merchant. Vincenzo really was a prince. Really knocked himself out. Made the happy couple feel special.

The meal was great and you couldn't beat the price."

"I'm not surprised to hear that at all," Jim said. "I've been coming here for years. Brought my parents here, the whole bit. Like you said, he goes out of his way to make you feel comfortable. Vinnie even gives me a few sauceless meatballs in a doggy-bag for Anakin."

"I love that. Hey, he's smart. Keep your customers happy and they'll come back."

Jim had to agree.

Joe leaned forwards towards Jim.

"We were speaking of the ticket my brother-in-law got in Corona. I think I mentioned I walked a beat there when Moses wore short pants. North Corona is still considered under the auspices of my precinct, the 115. Do you know the area at all? You ever get to Queens?"

"I really don't get to Queens much anymore," Jim said. "I used to work at a smaller firm in Elmhurst, which isn't too far from the area that you're talking about. I know it fairly well. But I haven't been there for quite some time. Probably years. My job keeps me tied up. Also, my brother was killed in that general location of Queens. Too many painful memories I don't wish to re-visit." Jim grimaced.

Joe eyes dropped to his belt, scanned the ceiling, then fixed on Jim.

"I wasn't aware of the area where your brother had been killed. I'm sorry."

"No apology necessary."

Vincenzo arrived with their dinners to break the mood, which was deteriorating into gloom and somberness.

Both men began eating, followed by a minute or two of uncomfortable silence. Their last exchange had taken some of the lightheartedness out of the evening and neither wanted to go down the dark alley of memory lane tonight.

Jim was halfway through his rigatoni with meatballs and wished to break the awkwardness. "Anyway, Joe, how is the hunt going to catch your killer?"

Joe put down his fork, wiped his mouth and took a sip of water. "I would love to say that our task force has made more headway, but sadly I can't. Believe me, it's not for lack of effort or any level of incompetence. I hate to say it but this guy's really good. Very smart. He's given us virtually nothing to go on. We're really up against it."

Jim grimaced. "I feel for you, I really do."

"We're starting to feel the heat, and the flames are coming from all sides. You read the papers, watch TV, go online, stay informed, you know what's going on. The public has gone from our cheering section to the idea that we are either (a) incompetent or (b) corrupt, in that we're protecting one of our own. It's not a good situation."

Vincenzo came over to bus the table and offer coffee, but both men passe. He left the check and two York Peppermint Patties. Next to that was a small brown paper bag that Jim guessed contained two meatballs without sauce, to be used as a late-night snack for Anakin. He opened the bag to show Joe and they both laughed.

"Let me get the check," volunteered Joe. "It was my invitation."

"That wouldn't be right. You and Patty have had me over for dinner a few times. Please, let me reciprocate, even if Patty couldn't make it tonight. And believe me, the cooking here is much better than anything that comes out of my kitchen."

Joe scratched under his right collarbone. "I know you attorneys are famous for your corner cutting, but the NYPD still takes a dim view of largesse. Let's save the headache and split it."

"Surprisingly fair and logical, especially from a civil servant." Jim felt the mood had now brightened. "Fine by me."

Following a thank you to their host for a great meal and the gift of meatballs, the two men headed home.

"I need to walk off that meal," Joe said. "I usually don't

eat that heavy at night."

"I need to walk to Jersey. I'm stuffed. But the food is great."

"No question."

Jim wanted to pursue what they'd been speaking about prior to Vinnie's coffee offer but was reticent to do so. The subject might be buried for the night as far as Joe was concerned. Jim was unable to read his neighbor's present body language and mood to determine his reaction to a question about an investigation that wasn't going very well. But he decided there was nothing to lose and took a shot. "I'm not trying to beat a dead horse, but has your team had any good leads?"

"We've had a few, but none really went anywhere. A few people were brought in, but nothing ever came of it. It's strange. So different than the usual homicide investigations. You know, murder over lust, greed, revenge, drugs, whatever. But you could figure the guy out, his motive. He would always slip up someplace, leave physical evidence, DNA, something. At the very least I always had a starting point that I could work from. But this is a whole new ballgame. We've got no real motive. I have to admit it's been tough on us. You hear about these guys who kill for years, bodies found all over the goddamn place before any breaks. I just pray we aren't in the midst of that right now."

Jim was surprised at his friend's frankness. This was more than just being honest. It was an admission that the police were stumped and not anywhere close to an arrest or even a strong suspect. He sympathized with Joe's dire situation, especially given the tragedy he endured.

"Well, maybe something will break soon for you. I'll keep good thoughts."

Joe quickened his pace. "Funny you should say that. And I appreciate the good wishes. I didn't say so before, but I developed a small lead that's worth pursuing. It may wind up being nothing, but I think it's worth my time. I'll keep you informed as to my progress, if you'd like me to do so."

"Yes, of course, that would be great, if it wouldn't be too inconvenient." Jim lengthened his stride to keep up with Joe. "Good luck. I hope it goes somewhere. Is there a chance you could share anything with me?"

"Well, my boss and I had the pleasure this morning of speaking with Alex Ortiz junior and his dad at their house. They're both freakin' hot-heads."

Jim said, "I've met them. The kid's a total loud-mouth jerk, and his dad's impossible to deal with."

Joe's eyes widened, and he slowed a bit to face Jim. "How'd you come in contact with those two?"

"The first time was a few years back at a charity softball event. There were attorneys and politicians at the game. The councilman and his kid both played. Junior was in arguments with fans, opponents, teammates, the umpire and the guy selling ice cream. A complete jackass. The dad could care less about his son's behavior."

Joe's cell phone buzzed. He spoke to the caller, without saying his name, for about thirty seconds. "Sorry, Jim. Go on."

"The second time was last year. Junior got into some 'alleged' criminal trouble, and my boss, Bill Dunn handled the case. The councilman and our senior partner Douglas White are friends, which in no way shocks me. But the victim dropped the charges. The rumor was that the councilman had paid her a small fortune, but my boss never confirmed that. I was in a few meetings with Ortiz and his son. They were both intolerable. To be blunt, senior is an excitable bully, and junior is an entitled and lazy bastard."

"Yeah, that's the impression I got from them today," Joe said. "At least their behavior is consistent."

"Do you think these two are involved in some way in the murders?" Jim asked.

"You never know. The kid got pissed at some of my questions, and the dad was so defensive. He went nuts. He essentially kicked us out. Their behavior is very suspicious and raises red flags."

"Listen, Joe. I don't want to be presumptuous, and I'm no crime fighter. But I know what it's like to lose someone you love, and I'd really like to help in the investigation, even in a small way. Is there anything I can do?"

"I know you lawyers all wanna be cops."

"I'm serious. Please, call on me if you need to. Even just to bounce ideas off or just vent."

"I appreciate it. At this point, I'm not sure. Let me give it some thought. Maybe I can put that shyster brain to good use."

"It hasn't been of any use for some time. Honestly, think about it."

Joe put his hands on his hips and bent backwards to stretch. "Ok, I will."

He thanked Jim for a much-needed night out and Jim thanked him for the invitation. The detective ascended his driveway, and the attorney did the same two houses down, disappearing into the dark.

Chapter 27

The following day Joe arrived at the Command Center as he had done each day for the past three months. But he had a feeling this day would be different. On the ride, he pondered last night's interaction with James Bradley. He had an opportunity or two to ask probing questions, but he eschewed them. The detective wanted to ask his neighbor if he varied his walk and extended it one night a month for the past 13 months, but had neither the nerve, nor the evidence at present. That could change in the near future.

Upon walking into the precinct, he saw a face he hadn't seen before. It belonged to a small, thin man with salt and pepper hair, a short graying beard and wire rimmed glasses.

This individual was standing between Brenner and Hollander. The three men stopped chatting as they realized Joe was now in the room. Joe dropped his briefcase at his desk and joined The Three Amigos.

Brenner spoke first. "Joe, I want to introduce you to Inspector Kenneth Ferguson."

Joe had heard of the good inspector. His reputation was that of a solid, yet unspectacular, cop. Through some hard work, good breeding and test scores, along with a close relationship with Commissioner Fields, he'd risen to the position of inspector, which in the NYPD is two ranks above captain. Joe was not sure why Mr. Ferguson was present at the 115 this fine morning.

He extended his hand. "Glad to meet you, Inspector. What brings you to our little nuthouse?"

"Pleasure is mine, Detective," Ferguson smiled and shook Devlin's hand firmly.

Brenner cleared his throat. "Let me just cut in here for a moment. Joe, this is on me, and I apologize for not keeping you in the loop. Late last night the Commissioner called me to advise that Inspector Ferguson would be joining us on the Task Force. I should've reached out to you earlier, but it's been one of those days already. I'm sorry that this situation wasn't handled better."

Joe wasn't certain how to respond since he wasn't certain what Inspector Ferguson's role would be. This had been Joe's operation from Day One. The brass had been supportive but weren't an every-day presence. FBI Agent Hollander had taken a hiatus to solve some killings somewhere in the Windy City. Up to this point, Joe and his people had carried the ball and the water. Besides, Inspector Ferguson had a background in administration, not "nuts and bolts" street work and investigations. Joe was baffled. He hoped his narrowed eyes weren't revealing his inner thoughts.

"I don't want to speak out of turn here, but what will the inspector be responsible for on the Task Force?" he asked.

"We feel, and the Commissioner does as well," Brenner said, "that we may not be optimizing your talents. We may have erred in keeping you in here so many hours of this investigation and not out on the streets where your great instincts can be maximized."

Joe didn't wish to minimize their maximize and felt as if he were at an Amazon stockholders meeting or Wall Street boardroom. When cops start talking optimizing and maximizing, he knew he was in trouble. Admittedly, Joe *was* in the Command Center coordinating activities within the investigation, but he'd spent his fair share of time on the street. He was hoping Brenner would soon be bringing his plane in for a landing.

"The public is getting antsy, as you can understand," Brenner said. "And we have to be sensitive and receptive to that. We truly feel that the Task Force will be more effective if Inspector Ferguson mans the Control Center and, in turn, you'd be freed up from some of these administrative hassles and headaches, enabling you to give the street its full concentration. I need your bulldog investigatory skills and determination out there. This isn't a demotion, merely a different method in which to allocate resources. Commissioner Fields believes this decision plays to both of your strengths. Hollander and I have tried to get Ken up to speed as much as possible. We were hoping you could fill in the rest of the blanks."

Well, he finally got there, even if he avoided the express lane. Brenner was a smart cop who was obviously forced by Commissioner Fields to be the one to share this decision. And he handled it well. In truth, Joe couldn't say it was a bad idea. Ferguson was a strong coordinator, while Joe was a strong investigator. So it made sense. It still felt like a demotion.

"Listen, Joe, I'm not here to step on anyone's toes," Inspector Ferguson said. "You're the lead investigator of the Task Force. I'm stepping into an administrative role. This is certainly not a comment on anyone's work performance. I just want to help out, be part of your team and contribute. I'm not looking to be a hero here. We all know this has been tough and we're up against it. This guy has to be taken off the streets, and if this way works, we should give it a shot."

Joe admired Ken's thoughts and cooperative spirit. The fact was that everyone in the room knew that their investigation had been impotent and ineffective, so it would seem self-serving if Joe objected to a different approach before giving it a chance.

"Glad to have you aboard, Inspector," Joe acquiesced. "We could use a shot in the arm right now. A different set of eyes and ears just may help. I need about five minutes to get organized, then I'll finish where Harry and Russell left off in their briefing."

"Sounds great, Joe, and please, call me Ken."

"Okay, Ken, see you in a few and we'll press on."

"You got it."

Joe pressed his lips together, then retreated to his desk in preparation for the transfer of many of his duties on the Task Force. Ferguson advised him that he needed to make a quick phone call and that he'd be right back. Joe wondered if the call was to the commissioner to beg the hell off the Task Force, or to his bookie, his girlfriend in Long Island City or Foo Luck Kitchen down the block.

This new role in the Task Force could work to Joe's advantage, he thought. His prior night's walk and meal with Jim Bradley revealed little, but his intuition told him not to dismiss his neighbor as a suspect. Before he could get himself to very seriously consider that possibility, and actually share it with the team, he needed much more information. None of it made sense, but it was still feasible. His stomach pains advised him not to give up on Ortiz senior and junior as suspects.

Since Joe lead the Task Force, he hadn't been assigned a partner. Without anyone to shadow his moves and without the everyday need to be at the Command Center any longer, Joe would be freed up to explore his three best suspects. He was sure that Brenner, after forcing Ferguson on him, wouldn't have the inspector hassle him with a lot of inquiries about his day-to-day whereabouts. Joe would be present at the Command Center on most days and would apprise Ferguson accordingly.

He had reservations about doing it this way, of going rogue in a sense. Joe felt a little guilty about keeping this from the team, but the time wasn't right yet. He felt even guiltier about suspecting Jim Bradley, who'd suffered in his own right. Joe had no appetite to probe into his neighbor's life, but the fact-finding went where it went.

A potential minefield was re-interviewing the Ortiz boys. The councilman had called the commissioner immediately after slamming the door in the face of the detectives to express his displeasure. It would take a lot of wheel-greasing to get another crack at father and son. The councilman had a powerful friend and ally in Mayor Louise Simpson. She wore many hats, the largest one being Commissioner Fields' boss. Joe could get jammed up in an effort to re-interview, and he didn't have the hard evidence at present to warrant a second bite at the Ortiz apple.

He closed his eyes in a futile attempt to keep these notions and images from rolling around in his head like a marble. Joe wasn't ready to deal with all of this right now. The detective had formulated an endgame, but things had to be done in their proper order. First, he needed a cigarette. Second, he needed a very large and very sweet cup of coffee. Third, he had to find Ken and catch him up to speed. There was no fourth, but if Joe had his druthers, it would include a winning lotto ticket and a sunny beach.

Chapter 28

Inspector Ferguson completed his first week at the helm of the Task Force as the calendar turned to February. Joe remained an integral part of the team, just as Brenner had promised. Ferguson had turned out to be a decent guy. He was a first-rate administrator, and let the men pursue their leads and investigate. In addition, he didn't poke his nose into Joe's day-to-day business.

Unfortunately, during the week, a fourteenth victim had been discovered. The partially decomposed body was found by a construction worker clearing a wooded lot.

Joe was sitting in his car down the block from the Command Center, a cinnamon roll in his left hand, a Dunkin' Donuts cup in his right. After his breakfast was quickly devoured, he needed a smoke. It was a cold morning, but he had his window open to exhale the nicotine and inhale the piercing air. The detective hoped the frosty draft would either provide clarity or wake him up.

He leaned his head back, closed his eyes and saw three suspects spinning their legs on a habitrail. All three, Bradley, Ortiz and Ortiz jr., made sense on some level, and no sense on another. Joe had been dissuaded by Brenner to re-interview the councilman and his son, fearing that a repeat performance could turn their pension into a box of kitty litter. The detective had been dragging his feet regarding Bradley, working up the nerve to ask him probing and pressing questions.

The detective glanced at his watch. He flicked his Marlboro onto the pavement below his car window and headed to his precinct. On the way he hoped he'd be hit with divine inspiration.

As it turned out divine inspiration *did* hit him. He had just sat down at his desk when Captain Sterling approached with Brenner a step behind. Sterling put his cell phone into his pocket, took off his glasses and cleaned them with a handkerchief.

"We have a situation, Joe."

"Did my *National Geographic* magazine get mailed to the office again?"

"I wish I had time for light-hearted discussion, but I don't. I just got off the phone with Commissioner Fields. You and Brenner are to report to 1PP immediately."

"Why, Captain, what's going on?"

"I'm just telling you what I was told. He hung up before I could ask. But I wouldn't go there expecting a promotion."

"I'll bring the car around," said Brenner.

"Thanks. Be right down." He turned toward Sterling, who wore a scowl as a princess wears a tiara. "We'll contact you after we know what's up."

"I know you will. Now get going."

With that Joe and Harry made their way to the commissioner's office. The traffic was fairly light as it was late morning. They rode in silence for about ten minutes.

Joe broke the ice. "What are you thinking, Harry?"

"Nothing good. Being summoned to 1PP in the middle of this investigation wasn't on my agenda this morning. Sterling told me the commissioner was irate on the phone, so I'm not thinking he wants our input on the holiday party."

"The captain didn't get that far with me," Joe said. "He just said the commish hung up before going into any details, so I'm guessing that his bulls-eye is on me. Your presence is to deter Fields from going for my throat. Besides, he didn't request that Ferguson come down to the principal's office."

Harry sped up to pass a car that was on a sight-seeing tour. "Let's not get ahead of ourselves," he said. "This may just be a situation where the commissioner wants information directly from us, rather than from intermediaries. Ferguson

has only been here a week. We've been with the Task Force
going on four months now. In his mind, it's the two of us
who are responsible to provide answers. But we're not
necessarily his targets."

"Sure, and Martin Scorsese wants me for his next movie."

Chapter 29

Brenner pulled into the parking garage at police headquarters. As they began walking toward the elevators, he turned to Joe.

"Maybe I should do most of the talking. I was supposed to do that at the councilman's house last month. It didn't work out, and we got jammed up. Okay, fine, I can live with that. We're after a serial killer, and you did what you felt you had to do. But this is different. This is politics and ass covering. Not your arena. If your temper gets the best of you with the commissioner, with the mood he's in, you could wind up in a jackpot. We both could."

Joe nodded his head. "I hear you. I'm gonna play nice. You *should* take the lead. You're better at it and Fields has a better relationship with you. I'm here to provide any information and details he wants, not to make waves. We're all angry that we haven't gotten the guy yet."

"Good, Joe. As long as we're on the same page and stay there."

"Copy that."

They were met at the elevator by the deputy commissioner and escorted to his office. The second in command was a thick, dapper man in his late fifties with a deep voice.

Fields had his hands in his pockets and was staring out his fourteenth-floor window. He massaged the back of his neck and turned to face his two detectives. He made direct eye contact and motioned to two chairs in front of his desk. "Please sit."

Brenner and Devlin silently took their seats, as if they were in a church pew. The commissioner sat down, folded his arms on top of his desk, leaned in and glared at his detectives. His blue three-piece suit, crisp white shirt and deep red tie gave him a patriotic and authoritative look. Devlin saw the crease in his forehead and flaring nostrils and wondered when this interminable staring contest would end.

The commissioner said, "Earlier this morning I got a visit from an extremely distraught and irate Councilman Alex Ortiz. When he returned home last night, he found his son dead in his room of an apparent overdose. I'm not sure at this time if it was accidental or not. The point is he blames the NYPD generally, and you specifically, Joe, for Alex junior's death."

Joe tilted his head to one side, his mouth half open. This was the last thing he expected to hear. As much he disliked both father and son, he couldn't fight off his feelings of empathy for a man who lost his son, just as he had. "I'm really sorry to hear about this. It's tragic and very unfortunate, but why does the councilman blame us?"

"He claims you browbeat his son when you interviewed, or should I say, interrogated him. That you hounded and accused an emotionally fragile young man who had turned his life completely around."

Joe tried to keep his nostrils from flaring. "With all due respect, that's an exaggerated summary of my interaction with his so-called model citizen son. As Detective Brenner knows, a former snitch named Clayton Taggart told me that Ortiz junior had discussed his possible role in the murders with a friend of Taggart, named Everett Michaels. Both Taggart and Michaels are now dead with possible drug ties. Junior was a former, or should I say current, user. Until last night of course. I had every reason to go at the kid. I've interrogated perps for years and was a hell of a lot harder with them than I was with the kid. It didn't rise to an improper or inappropriate level. Harry witnessed the entire conversation."

Brenner inspected his fingernails and chewed on a cuticle.

"Yes, Commissioner, we were both in Councilman Ortiz's house as part of our investigation. When I came to you for the o.k., after Joe had told me about the information he'd gotten from his former informant, you agreed it was worth a conversation. We may not have treaded as lightly as we could have, but Joe was never out of bounds. It got heated, yes. But both father and son have quick tempers. And based on the direction of Joe's questions, it did appear that they weren't completely forthcoming and couldn't wait for us to go. As a matter of fact, the councilman threw us out."

Joe was impressed that Harry had not hung him out to dry. He wanted to add to Harry's defense of his actions, but the commissioner put up his right hand in Joe's direction. He then placed his fingertips together, peering at the steeple he had created.

"I've known Ortiz for a long time," the commissioner said. "He's a good politician, very smart and very tough. His constituents love him. But he's a hot-headed boil on my butt, and his good for nothing son has been in trouble since he was in diapers, may he rest in peace. Our mayor, who I serve at the pleasure of, is a staunch supporter of Ortiz. Based on my prior dealings with councilman and son, and my respect for you, Joe, I'm inclined to believe that you were doing your job as best you could, investigating and trying to clear this case."

Joe quietly exhaled. "That's all that it was. have no ax to grind with either father or son, and I genuinely feel badly about the kid's death. But I have to go where the trail leads, and it led us to their home. I know the councilman has juice, and now with the death of his son, he'll be in Mayor Simpson's ear before lunch."

"Breakfast. She already called me. I was summoned to her office for an afternoon meeting. I needed your version before she got her hooks into me. Don't get me wrong, the mayor and I have a decent relationship, but she treats Ortiz like a favorite son. I'm in a no-win situation."

Brenner rubbed his temples. "Commissioner, how did you leave it with Ortiz?"

"I sympathize with him and understand he's grieving, but he was completely unreasonable. He wants to sue the NYPD; he wants Joe off the job, wants his badge. Apparently, his next stop after brightening my morning was going to be Mayor Simpson's office."

Brenner sat nodding his head. Joe tried to keep his interior alarm from buzzing. The thought of a lawsuit and possibly losing his badge and pension scared the crap out of him. Not to mention that his plan would be disrupted or possibly derailed.

The commissioner tapped his fingers on the desk. "I also appealed to his sense of civic responsibility. To the fact that we all want this maniac off the streets. Ortiz should be motivated to catch this guy because most of the victims resided in his district. But he wouldn't hear it. He also claims that he can provide an alibi for junior for each murder. He admonished me that our fishing expedition was not only worthless, but it cost his son's life. Then he stormed out. That's how we left it Harry."

"Is senior the alibi for junior?" Joe asked.

"I didn't peel the onion that far. He was making his point loudly, and I sensed that he wasn't in the mood for questions or give-and-take."

"Do you think we should pay a condolence call?" Harry asked.

The commissioner pressed his lips together. "Absolutely not. My deputy commissioner of public information will take care of any matters related to the son's death. You and Devlin are not to have any contact with the councilman. He specified that just before he graciously exited."

"I understand," Harry said.

Joe pulled at his jacket sleeve. "Please forgive me Commissioner, but I don't understand. I mean, I get it from your perspective, from the political angle, but the councilman is still a suspect. If he can go to the mayor for protection, and then she can close ranks, how can we do our jobs? We need to go back at him. I'll admit it must be done tactfully, but it has to be done. You said he alibis his son, but who can alibi him?"

The commissioner stroked his chin. "If we had something more concrete on him, something substantial and beyond just mere suspicions, I would tell you guys to run with it and let me handle the political fall-out. Joe, you told me that Taggart and Michaels are both dead, and both had drug histories and connections. Now Ortiz junior is dead, drug related. Do you actually think that the councilman killed fourteen people, killed Taggart and Michaels to shut them up, then killed his own son?"

Joe scratched the back of his left shoulder with his right hand. "Phrased like that I know it seems far-fetched. But maybe he killed the fourteen victims, but the other three deaths were actually suicides, or accidental overdoses. That's not completely unreasonable. There are a few things that point to him, but we only got one crack at him and now he is using the mayor to shield him from further questioning.

"He's still worth a look, I agree," Brenner said. But, like you said commissioner, we don't have any real evidence to confront him with, even if we were permitted to confront him."

The commissioner jotted down a note, folded it in half, and slid it into his inside jacket pocket. "Here's the deal. I'll meet with the mayor and assure her that we'll continue to pursue all possible leads, and that the councilman will not be harassed by the NYPD. You two are authorized to collect evidence pertaining to any reasonable suspect, including the councilman. But this must be done without contacting him or anyone in his close circle. Put your ear to the streets. Shake a few trees and see what falls out. Bring anything regarding Ortiz directly to me. I'll advise Captain Sterling and Lt. Moss. Please brief Inspector Ferguson on this protocol." He turned to Joe. "I don't want any rogue activity, Detective."

"Yes, Commissioner, I don't either."

"Good day detectives, and good luck. I'll speak to you soon."

The deputy commissioner opened the door to signal it was time for their departure. He had entered right on cue. Joe figured he'd heard every word from his office due to a highly placed buddy in the IT department.

On the ride back to the precinct, Harry adjusted the radio to an oldies station, then with one eye on the road and one on Joe, asked, "Any thoughts?"

"Plenty."

"Any you would like to share?"

"Not right now. But soon."

Chapter 30

James Bradley had just stepped out of the shower when the phone rang. He raced to answer it, having to step over Anakin on his route. It was the Friday before President's Day weekend and he and his sister-in-law Michelle were going skiing. The week had been stressful, and he was looking forward to their weekend getaway. He answered the phone with his left hand, running a towel through his hair with his right.

"Hello."

"Hi, Jim. Please don't be mad, but I think I'm going to pass on the ski trip. I know it's last minute, but my heart isn't in it."

"Why, Michelle, did something happen? Are you alright?"

"I'm ok, I guess. I don't know. I haven't been skiing since David…well, you know. I wanted to get away from it all this weekend, but now I just feel blah."

David was a fantastic skier, and had taught Michelle, who had become a first rate one as well. They went skiing in upstate New York or Vermont often. They even ventured out to Colorado and Utah one year. Now, after all these years, Jim realized that Michelle still couldn't bring herself to engage in an activity she loved because it brought back painful memories.

"I understand. But I won't go without you."

"No, Jim, please go and enjoy yourself. I'll feel guilty if you cancel because of me."

"How can I go without you? Who will bring me to the infirmary and help me with my crutches?"

Michelle laughed. "Okay. As long as you don't mind."

"Let's get together anyway. We both took off, so let's have lunch. I'll pick you up around 1:00 p.m."

"I have to pick up something from the mall by your house. I can meet you there between 1:00 and 1:15," Michelle said.

"Sounds good. Bring your pocketbook in case I forget my wallet or go to the men's room when I see the waiter bringing the check."

"Klutzy and cheap is no way to go through life, Jim."

"Just playing the hand I was dealt."

Jim again had to face the reality that David's death had created great anxiety for not only he and his parents, but for Michelle also. He had never divulged to his sister-in-law that while in therapy, Dr. Lawrence had been exploring the idea that Jim was repressing the feeling that his parents were closer with his brother, that they loved him more.

"Do you feel like your parents favored David? Or perhaps following his death he rose to a place in their heart or to a status you could never attain?"

Dr. Lawrence's questions had irked Jim. "Look, doc, we all saw *Ordinary People* and understand the 'favorite son' complex. I chose to come to you because you talk sense and provide practical advice, not psychological mumbo jumbo from a textbook. I loved David very much and never ever resented anything about him. It's natural for parents who lose a child to remember him as being almost perfect. I get it."

"But Jim, I think it would be productive if we examined…"

Jim had held up his left hand in a dismissive manner. "Stop, doc, I can't deal with this right now. Let's pick it up next time." Jim had abruptly ended that session and never returned.

Michelle pulled up in front of Jim's house about 10 minutes past one. Her face winced as the cold winter air struck it, and she smiled when she saw Jim waiting behind the glass door. She was wearing white sneakers and blue jeans. Her hooded black winter coat hid most of her gray sweater, except for the turtleneck part, which peeked out. The cold February day forced her to wear gloves, but she had eschewed a hat, so her wavy black hair blew in the afternoon breeze. She was able to hide the devastation that penetrated her heart and her soul from most, but Jim could see it as plain as a ski slope.

Jim opened the door for her, kissed her cheek and placed her coat on a chair at the dining room table. Anakin rumbled from his resting spot to greet Michelle. As he sniffed the air, he yelped and bounced toward her. She knelt and scratched him behind the ears and then gave the dog a lingering hug, pushing her nose into his smooth fur as Anakin happily licked his ear.

"Would you two like to be alone?"

"Don't be like that, Jim. Klutsy, cheap and jealous is no way to go through life."

They both laughed and moved to the living room where they sat on opposite sides of the sofa, with the Rottweiler occupying the middle.

Michelle fidgeted with the bracelet that David had given her their last Christmas together. "I'm really sorry about the last-minute cancellation. I should've called you last night. I hoped by the morning I'd feel different. But when I started to get ready, and took our suitcase out of the closet, it just hit me harder than I expected." Michelle's breaths quickened and her voice trailed off. Her last few words were barely audible. She squeezed her eyes shut and tears ran down her cheeks.

Jim reached for some tissues and offered them to her.

"I don't mind, really I don't. I wasn't in the mood to go either. I could use the three-day weekend to catch up on some sleep and work."

More composed, Michelle said "Thanks. You're always so sweet, just like your brother. Your parents raised you very well."

Jim wasn't quite sure how he felt about his mother and

father receiving the credit for the siblings' good behavior, but this was a poor time for a philosophical debate. "Are you ready for lunch?"

"Yes, I'm getting hungry."

"Good, what are you in the mood for? Chinese? Italian?"

"I'm more in a greasy burger and oily fries mood."

"Okay, you twisted my arm, Michelle. Burgers, fries and milk shakes it is. Pepto-Bismol for dessert." Jim pulled her coat from the chair and opened it up for Michelle to slide into. "We'll take my car."

They walked toward the door with Anakin trailing them. Jim said, "I'm sorry, buddy, you have to stay home. I'll take you for a walk tonight."

Anakin laid down, his massive head resting on his wide paws. Michelle knelt to give him a peck on the head. "We'll bring you back something."

Jim opened the door, but suddenly remembered he forgot Michelle's gloves on the table and went to retrieve them. Anakin had stealthily snuck behind them, and seeing a familiar face outside, uncharacteristically bolted past Michelle and out of the house. She yelled his name loudly, and once Jim realized that what was going on he sprinted toward the door and outside, calling for his dog.

As he descended his porch, Jim gathered himself and controlled his breathing. Anakin's escape had stopped at the foot of the driveway. Joe was petting him. His dog looked happy, his neighbor looked happy, but a man Jim hadn't seen before accompanied Det. Devlin, and the color had drained out of the stranger's face. Jim hustled down the driveway to meet them, with Michelle a few steps behind.

Jim said, "I'm sorry, Joe, he's never done that before. He must have seen you and darted out. You know how much he likes you. I hope he didn't scare you."

"No, I'm fine Jim, and the feeling's mutual," Joe said. "But I'm not sure about my friend here." Joe extended his hand to Jim and said hello to Michelle. "It's very nice to see you again."

"Yes, it was nice for Anakin to get us all together again," Michelle said laughing.

Joe said, "This is my friend, Russell Hollander. We were walking and talking when your dog happened to join us. Russ, let me introduce Jim Bradley and his sister-in-law, Michelle. This is the family that I told you about, that Patty and I spent Thanksgiving with."

"Yes, I recall," Russell said. "In full disclosure I'm an FBI Agent. I've dealt with serial killers and kidnappers for years, but when I saw your dog racing towards us, I thought I was finished. Please don't tell my colleagues at Quantico."

Following a group laugh, Michelle said, "I know, he's a bit intimidating at first. But he's really a big lovable mush."

"Yes, once my heart started again, I realized that. He's very well behaved, and obviously has bonded with Det. Devlin."

Joe and Jim both shook their heads in agreement.

Michelle said, "Agent Hollander, may I ask you a question?"

"Sure, Ms. Wagner, and please call me Russell."

"Okay, and please make that Michelle. Russell, you mentioned your work with serial killers. I'm assuming that based seeing you with Detective Devlin that you're working with him to catch the person responsible for, what is it 14, murders?"

"Yes, Michelle, it is unfortunately 14 deaths, and the detective and I are both part of a task force."

"We wish you the best of luck. Those poor families. Such a tragedy. We understand what they're going through."

Russell looked sheepishly at Joe. "I hope you don't feel like I betrayed a trust," Joe said to Jim and Michelle, "but after our holiday together I told Russ about David's death."

Jim said, "No, not at all. It's fine." Michelle nodded her head in agreement.

Russell said, "I'm very sorry for the loss of your husband,

Michelle, and your brother, Jim. We see a lot of death in my business and my heart goes out to you as well Joe, for the loss of your son."

The chilly winter afternoon was suddenly filled with awkward silence, finally broken by Jim. "If I'm not prying or over-stepping, how is the investigation progressing? You may think this is odd, Russell, but I very much would like to help out in any way I can. I know a lot of judges. If you need any assistance with warrants or subpoenas, please feel free to call on me."

"We appreciate that very much," Russell said. "And we'll of course take that into consideration. Right now, we have a few suspects we're zeroing in on. Nothing definite, but we have some irons in the fire."

"We'll keep good thoughts for your team and the families," Jim said.

"Yes, God's speed, all the luck," said Michelle.

"Thanks," said Joe and Russ simultaneously.

They exchanged good-byes and good weekend wishes and continued on with their day. Jim and Michelle went out for lunch, and Joe and Russ stopped off at Joe's house on their way back to work.

Chapter 31

Joe was finishing dinner Sunday night when he heard the familiar buzzing sound of his cell phone. He wiped his hands on a napkin and quickly picked up.

"Hello, Harry. How was your weekend?"

"Not great. Sorry, but not in the mood to chat. I just got off the phone with the commissioner."

Sentences like Harry's last one reminded Joe of his childhood, when his parents would begin conversations with, "I just got off the phone with the principal" or "I just spoke to one of the store-owners." The next thing out of their mouth was generally something unpleasant. He assumed this situation was no different.

"What did he want, Harry?"

"Let's just say that he wasn't encouraging me to buy Girl Scout cookies from his daughter. The commissioner wants us to come to 1PP tomorrow for another visit. Fields was somewhere between terse and testy."

"Tomorrow is President's Day. Do you think he wants to discuss Washington and Lincoln?"

"I think he wants us on a spit."

"What now? Did the councilman make another beef? Or maybe the mayor is displeased and got irate with Fields at their meeting?"

"I'm not sure, Joe. It wasn't a long conversation, nor was our attendance presented as an option. Do you want to meet there or drive over together?"

This was like being asked if you prefer being stabbed or drowned.

Joe said, "We'll meet at the precinct then drive in together like last time. Hopefully the meeting will go better."

"Don't go to Vegas with that notion. See you tomorrow. Have a good night."

"Yeah, you too, Harry. See you then."

Patty heard Joe's end of the conversation as she cleared the table and wrapped the left-overs. "More trouble? My God, I hope not another killing."

"No, I don't think it's anything like that. The commissioner would've told Harry if that were so, and he would've told me. I'm not sure of the specifics. But when Ted Fields calls my boss, and we both have to trek in tomorrow, I wouldn't expect a Hawaiian vacation."

Patty sighed. "I pray every night for the families. But I see what this is doing to you. The sleepless nights, the agitation, the constant worry. All of this stress, and on top of what we went through with Thomas. How much more can you take?"

Joe's heart broke for his wife. Her once hardy and robust disposition had been supplanted by emotional fragility. Although she was visibly withered, Joe appreciated the strength she still provided him, and the solace she wished to bring to the victims' kin. "Not much more, Patty. Not much more."

Joe plopped into his recliner. In his mind, the list of suspects was down to two; Councilman Alex Ortiz and Jim Bradley, Esq. The detective was cognizant of the fact that no member of the task force knew that his neighbor was even on his radar. He and Harry had advised the commissioner during their prior meeting that the councilman was a possible suspect, but Joe had kept Jim's possible involvement to himself. When he and Russell had driven back to the precinct from his home, Joe briefly considered sharing his intel with the FBI agent, but he wasn't ready and wasn't sure he'd ever be. The plan he was formulating to get to his endgame didn't require him to share his gut-feeling that Jim Bradley was a suspect.

The following day Joe sat in the passenger seat as Harry

Brenner simultaneously drove, fiddled with the radio and mumbled to himself. Joe surmised he wasn't the only one being emotionally crushed by the weight of this investigation.

The detective stared out his window onto the FDR Drive. He was torn. He liked and respected his neighbor. Not to mention the heartache he and his family had endured.

The other suspect he disliked intensely and always had.

Ted Fields' Deputy of Public Information met them at the lobby elevators. Joe wanted to say, "Devlin, party of two, is our table ready?" But the DPI had the sense of humor of a butterless bagel, and Harry would have taken out his 9mm service pistol. Joe therefore avoided kowtowing to his whimsy.

Commissioner Fields was staring out of his 14th floor window onto Pearl Street, in the general direction of the East River. His hands were in his pockets and he had his back turned as the DPI ushered them in. As he faced them, Joe recognized the commissioner's traditional garb, a blue three-piece suit, crisp white shirt and Cardinal red tie. He put out his left hand, ostensibly to motion his two subordinates to the chairs facing his desk.

The commissioner took his seat, pushed his glasses toward his face with his left index finger and drew in a sharp breath. "We have a new development that needs to be talked through and some details to unpack."

Joe knew this "new development" was not going to create a warm and fuzzy ambiance in the office. A "new development" was akin to the "I just go off the phone with.." preamble, and what was sure to follow wouldn't be the blissful inner peace of the commissioner.

Harry said, "What is it Ted, what's going on?"

Joe thought but didn't say, "Yes, Ted, please make it quick and stop bothering us with nonsense."

"I'm sure you'll both recall that following our last meeting I was summoned to Mayor Simpson's office for what she called a conference, but a more appropriate term would be a bloodletting. In any case, she advised me that we should no longer consider Councilman Alex Ortiz a subject of our investigation."

An "Ugh" escaped from Joe's mouth, followed by a shudder.

Harry held up his right hand in Joe's direction. "Take it easy, Joe. Commissioner, on what basis are were dismissing Ortiz as a suspect?"

"I asked the same question, Harry. Remember, I was once a detective. The Mayor explained to me that she and the councilman have been involved in a relationship for the past several years, dating back to well before the first body was found. It's not exactly scandalous, as Ortiz is divorced and she never married, but this situation is ripe for conflict-of-interest issues. That's why they don't advertise it, and why they're very discreet, and also why it was *strongly* suggested that I share this only with a select few. You two are the few."

Joe realized he was wrong in his evaluation of the mayor-councilman relationship.

He thought Simpson treated Ortiz like a favorite son, but unless there was an Oedipal theme to their activities, Ortiz was literally the one who served at the mayor's pleasure.

"So why did she choose to include you in the inner sanctum?" Harry said. "Is her point that she can alibi him for 14 nights?"

"Yes, that's her position. That they've spent every night for the past several years together. She also claims that she was present at most, if not all, of the late night political functions attended by Ortiz. The mayor is very adamant that he couldn't be our guy."

Joe said, "Commissioner, with all due respect, she can assert this position all she wants, but how can we trust that she was forthright?"

"Again, I had the same concern." He handed papers to both men. "Please review these documents."

"What are they, Ted?" asked Harry.

"Reports from three independent companies that perform lie-detector tests. Two of which the NYPD uses. Both passed all of their polygraphs with flying colors. I think we have no choice but to declare Ortiz a dead-end. He needs to be crossed off our list of suspects."

Joe and Harry exchanged glances. Joe hated to admit defeat, but now any further investigation of the councilman would only be viewed as a waste of time and resources, and possibly as a senseless vendetta. Harry sat silently, the report in one hand, his forehead in the other.

Joe saw Harry slump in his chair. If he had to venture a guess it would be that Harry didn't know where to turn next to find the killer. Joe had an idea but didn't like considering it. At present, his neighbor was their only real suspect. This caused great anxiety for the detective, exacerbated by the fact that he had not clued in anyone about this clue.

The commissioner leaned forward in his chair, glaring at both men. "So to be clear, and so we're all in agreement, any consideration of Ortiz as a suspect, any exploration or examination into his life, will cease and desist *immediately.*"

Fields hurled the word immediately at them with high velocity. "At this point, it's completely unreasonable and irresponsible to pursue him. But that begs my next question, gentlemen, who is it that we can reasonably and responsibly pursue?"

Joe assumed this question was above his pay grade and was intended for Brenner. He hoped the chief of detectives could come up with an acceptable answer. Or even a plausible lie.

"The cupboard's certainly not bare, Commissioner," Harry said. "We have a few leads we're pursuing and following up on. Joe has a C.I. whose fed us some good intel, and there's a potential suspect we have to go back and take a look at. Also, our team has developed a possible witness to one of the murders. There's still many avenues to explore, Ted."

One of the Flying Wallendas couldn't have walked this tightrope better than Joe's boss just had. Harry had been purposely vague and had omitted certain facts. Such as, the C.I. referenced was no longer with them, the suspect turned out to be a blind alley and the witness wrapped his ears in aluminum foil to receive better TV reception.

The Joint Task Force Team's investigation of and dealings with Malcolm Sturgess, Clayton Taggart, Everett Michaels, Alex Ortiz Jr., Alex Ortiz Sr. and Gary Carpenter hadn't produced any hard evidence that could be used to solve the murders. After 14 months and 14 murders, the identity of the culprit was still unknown. Only Joe had an idea who it might be.

"Okay, Harry, I'll leave it in your hands," the commissioner said. "But the leash is getting shorter by the minute. We've got to get this guy and get this story off the front page. Let me know if you need any more resources. And keep me in the loop. We'll meet again in a week to discuss our progress."

Great, Joe thought. *Another trip to purgatory.* He felt further pressure to make an arrest just to avoid these field trips into the Big Apple.

"Very good, Commissioner," Harry said. "I'll brief Sterling, Ferguson and Moss when I return, and we'll communicate with your office as often as possible. Hopefully, we'll get some good news soon."

"We need good news yesterday, Harry," the commissioner said. "That's all. Have a productive day, gentlemen. We'll be speaking very soon.

Chapter 32

Following the surprising revelation regarding the relationship between Councilman Ortiz and Mayor Simpson, and learning that they'd passed numerous polygraphs, Joe had to accept the idea that he needed to ramp up his investigation of Jim Bradley. Although the thought of this bothered him, questions regarding the ticket his neighbor received on a Queens night was keeping him up. He still preferred to tackle the scrutinizing of his neighbor's life alone. This newfound rogue mentality was contrary to his experience and training, but he felt it was justified.

During the course of the next several weeks, the detective had been able to accomplish his goal of studying and analyzing the comings and goings of Jim Bradley, without interference from the other members of the task force. Ostensibly, Joe remained part of the team, but with Inspector Ferguson being brought onboard to coordinate and supervise, Joe had the opportunity to act independently without the prying eyes of colleagues. Ferguson never poked his nose into Joe's day-to-day business.

Hence, neither Ferguson nor Brenner nor any other team member was aware that Devlin had been conducting an independent surveillance of his neighbor and friend. This exploration and observation of Jim's life began at the end of February.

Most, if not all, of Joe's investigation transpired after Jim came home from work. Bradley took the same train each morning. On an occasional random day, he'd catch a later one. He was usually home by 7:00 p.m. during the week. Weekends of course were different since Jim didn't go into

Manhattan for work. Joe didn't spend a lot of time observing Jim during the weekends for two reasons. First, he felt it was riskier, and didn't want to arouse suspicion or tip Jim off. Second, none of the victims were killed on a weekend, so Joe concentrated his efforts on the weekday nights.

By the mid-March, Joe decided that he needed assistance. Instead of availing himself of police resources, he brought in his brother-in-law to help. While he had great consternation about including Sam, Joe felt he had no choice. Their phone conversation started out very generally.

Sam said, "Just listening to some Mozart. I know he's your favorite. Elizabeth went to the store. What are Patty and you up to today?"

"Going out for an early lunch soon, then I have to get back to work. This case is a freakin' bear."

"I hope you get this guy soon, for everyone's sake. It's a shame there's not a way for me to help out. You were so gracious in handling my ticket, I feel I owe you a favor."

"Funny thing is, I think there's a way you can help me. But it would have to be strictly confidential. Patty and Elizabeth couldn't ever know. It's not something I can get into over the phone. There's no real danger involved, but you'll be performing investigatory tasks, and you must be very discreet. If you're in, let me know. If not, this subject was never broached and will be dropped forever, with absolutely no hard feelings."

"Well, I'm a partner in an accounting firm, which isn't exactly a vocation full of risks and close calls. I'd love to be useful but can't deal with shootouts or high-speed chases."

Joe laughed. "I promise there'll be none of that. But just be honest with me. If you can't, you can't. Or if you need some time to mull it over, that's fine."

"No, Joe. I don't need more time. I can do it around my work schedule. We're swamped this time of year, but I'm in."

"That's great. Come by the house tomorrow around 8:00

p.m. and we'll go down to the basement to watch TV and talk, that way Patty will think it's one of our usual get-togethers."

"Fine, see you then."

"Thanks, Sam."

With that Sam Weiss had joined the Task Force, only Harry Brenner, Kenneth Ferguson and the rest of the group weren't made aware of that fact.

By mid-April, Sam had been working with Joe for about a month. Joe had explained the route that he and Jim had walked the night they ate at the Leaning Tower of Pizza, and asked Sam to park his car in random spots to see if Jim consistently walked that same route. Joe figured that Jim might recognize his car parked on the street or in a parking lot, but that he wouldn't be able to identify Weiss' car. Weiss kept a detailed and neatly compiled log of Jim's activities. On nights Sam wasn't available, Joe would park his car in a more remote location and watch Jim, or even "accidentally" run into him while he was on one of his walks. The two laughed at the coincidence and finished the walk together.

Joe and his brother-in-law now had this down to a science, but for all their efforts so far it yielded nothing. Jim was like clockwork. He left his home on foot at around eight or eight thirty p.m. each night, and returned home roughly at ten, give or take.

There was one night the previous month when he came home much later than usual, but Joe dismissed it as an aberration because the killing was in Queens and Joe was on foot in Long Island. Maybe he went to someone's house, got a slice at the Leaning Tower, something like that. The odd thing about it was that the only night of March that Jim returned home much later than normal happened to be the same night that a 15th body was discovered behind a vacant warehouse in Corona. Maybe Joe's dismissal was premature.

With Sam tied up with a crisis at work and him stuck

home tending to Patty's flu, Joe was only able to observe the time Jim left and when he returned home. Nothing in between. But Joe was sure he left on foot and returned on foot, many hours later. Joe's experience told him to hang in a little longer with Bradley, but his logic and his lumbago made him feel as if he was losing his marbles.

Eventually, in late April, Joe got the break he desperately needed. It turned out that his experience trumped his logic, and his lumbago. Joe had borrowed a friend's vehicle and was parked stealthily between two SUVs on Liberty Blvd. Jim always walked past Maury's bagels onto Breyer, where the Leaning Tower of Pizza stood proudly. But on this particular night, instead of making a right on Liberty, he made a left and headed north until he walked out of Joe's sight.

Nassau County wasn't like Manhattan or Brooklyn where cars are parked everywhere and every which way, and the main traffic condition was gridlock. In the suburbs, traffic was sparser, especially after the evening rush hour. Joe had to be extra cautious to avoid detection.

The detective had situated his car in a secluded spot and now saw Jim walking on Post Ave. until he reached Railroad Ave. *Was he going on the train?* Jim walked toward the enormous Long Island RailRoad parking lot. Joe moved his car slowly, keeping a fair distance, acting as if he was looking for a parking spot. Finally, Jim found the car he was looking for, a gray Honda Accord. It looked to Joe like the same car that Jim had been driving the night he received a speeding ticket in Corona. The car that he'd learned was registered to Michelle Wagner, Jim's sister-in-law.

Jim slid behind the steering wheel and started the car. He looked down at something for about a half a minute then took off. Joe was blindsided by this parking lot detour and wasn't sure if he should follow him or not. It was almost 9:00 p.m. and there weren't many cars driving in the train parking lot at the time. If Jim saw Joe, he'd have a hard time explaining his actions. He waited for Jim to exit the parking lot and followed a good distance behind. Jim headed for the Long Island Expressway. As he veered to the right for the westbound LIE onramp, Joe stayed straight and passed it by. He pulled into in a 7-11 parking lot.

Joe needed a few minutes to process the events of the last hour. He remembered that on Thanksgiving Michelle had told Patty and him that she worked overnight as a nurse at New York County Hospital. That meant she probably was on a train into Penn Station in Manhattan sometime around 8:00 p.m. Joe surmised that it wasn't unreasonable that Jim would have a key to his sister-in-law's car. What Joe didn't know was if Michelle was aware that her brother-in-law was taking her car one night a month, and for what purpose he needed it? Joe put on his glasses and quickly jotted down some questions and thoughts in a small spiral pad. Next, he called his old partner.

"Hello, Joey, great to hear from you. Hope you're calling about a case that's being closed."

"Hi, Al, sorry to bother you, and no, not quite."

"Sorry to hear it, but it's good to shoot the breeze with you."

"Not just calling for that, Al. I need a little help. I know you have a whole bunch of cop buddies who work in Corona and Elmhurst, in those areas."

"Yeah, sure I do. Lots. Worked there myself for years, with you. What can I do? Is this something for the case?"

"It could be, but nothing concrete. See if your guys can head off or detain a gray Honda." Joe proceeded to provide Al with the license plate and driver information.

"Are we talking APB stuff here, Joe?"

"No, I need something less formal. Have your guys in those areas pull him over, for any reason. Tell him his car was reported stolen, there's criminal activity in the area, anything to chase him back to Long Island."

"And then what?"

"I'll take it from there. Tell your guys no rough stuff or BS, and I'll take care of all of them, including you."

"You know I'm not about that, Joe."

"I meant Polident or diapers."

"You're still a hump. Let me get on it and get back to you."

"Thanks, Al. Again."

Joe hung up his call and went inside for some coffee, crumb cake and sanity. This whole thing was crazy. His next call should have been to Brenner, Ferguson or Hollander, but he held off on that for now. He returned to his car and waited for Al's call.

About ten minutes later, Joe was polishing off his coffee when Al called to advise that the appropriate people had been contacted and the appropriate message sent. Joe thanked Al for his aid and told him he would wait for a future call.

Joe backed his car into a different parking spot, lit a cigarette, and blew the smoke out the window. He leaned his head back, put his right hand to his forehead and closed his eyes. His left hand was holding his Marlboro between his index and middle fingers, his left arm bent at the closed window. Joe was fairly certain that he was zeroing in on the serial killer, yet he wasn't overcome with a feeling of satisfaction or pride. Rather, a numbness crept into his psyche, a sensation he'd experienced many times since his son had been murdered. He hadn't expected that at this moment. Another thought penetrated his mind, one he knew shouldn't be present. Still, it would require attention. He had experienced this feeling before, despite his efforts to dismiss it. He knew it had to be addressed at some point. Joe flicked his cigarette onto the parking lot pavement.

A buzzing woke Joe from a catnap, groggy and irritable.

"Hi, Al, any news."

"Yeah, but nothing earth shattering. The Honda was already on the LIE heading east your way when my guy spotted him. He called me but I told him forget it. I hope that was okay. I figured if the guy was already headed back your way, why break his balls? Was that kosher?"

"Sure, that was fine. I'll catch up with him later. Thanks again."

"Anytime, Joe. Wanna clue me in on what's going on?"

"Soon, Al. Promise. Have a good night. Get some rest before your prostate starts barking."

"You always knew how to express appreciation. Be well, my friend."

Joe had hoped to catch Jim Bradley prior to him engaging in any "activity," but if he was heading home, they may've been too late. With no more need for the 7-11 menu or spacious parking he headed home.

Patty was already sleeping when Joe entered their bedroom. His wife's once beautiful face was worn and exhausted. She was thinner, and the once delicate skin under her eyes was sunken and hollow. With eyes closed, he recalled the moment that they'd found out their son had been murdered. He'd failed in his attempts to suppress this memory.

Patty had just checked the oven to evaluate the progress of her chicken and potatoes. Soon dinner would be ready, but her son wasn't home yet. "He's never late, Joe. Where could he be? You should have picked him up after practice."

"He wanted to walk home with Andy Benton. Thomas isn't a kid anymore, Patty. Most of the other kids walk home themselves. The field's a short walk away."

A half hour later a burnt meal sat on the table. Patty called Mrs. Benton to find out if Andy was home. She told Patty that Andy was picked up after practice by his aunt. They'd offered Thomas a ride home, but he'd elected to walk.

Patty hung up slowly, fixated on the wall above the phone. The color drained out of her face and her lower lip quivered. The detective's cell phone buzzed. Joe answered hurriedly.

"Detective Devlin." The voice on the other end, a Nassau

County homicide detective, delivered the news that would alter their lives forever. Thomas Devlin's stabbed body had been found at the exit of the woods near Sanders parkway. Right behind Bailey's auto shop, where Joe brought their cars for service.

Joe wanted to scream into the phone, "You must've made a mistake. My son can't be dead. It's someone else's poor kid that was found." He was in denial, heading toward anger. He turned his back to Patty as a tear shimmered in his eye. She sprinted to answer the house phone. Joe turned his attention back to his cell caller.

"I'm so sorry for your loss, Detective. Please accept our condolences. We caught the guy. His name's Keith Jenkins. He's a drug addict and child molester."

Joe said, "Was my son…well, I mean, was Thomas…?"

"No, it doesn't appear so, Detective. His clothes were torn a bit. Jenkins may have tried but heard something or someone, panicked and fled. But we arrested the bastard."

"Thank you, Detective." Joe said. We appreciate your efforts."

"Again, we're so sorry for your loss. I'll keep your family in my prayers."

Joe ended his call just as Patty hung up the house phone. He fought the urge to put his fist through the kitchen window, or to go Keith Jenkins holding cell and gut him like a mackerel. He tried to prepare his face before turning to her. His mouth opened but nothing came out. The detective was fighting a losing battle in holding back tears.

Patty screamed out, "No, Joe, no. Please God no, not Thomas, not my baby." She buried her face in her hands, her sobs becoming louder and uncontrollable. As Joe approached, she began banging on the wall, until he hugged her and pinned her arms to her sides. She slumped against him, collapsing into his arms. They both sank slowly to the floor, their bodies squeezed together.

Joe re-opened his eyes. He dropped a kiss on Patty's cheek

and quietly went into his study, where the upstairs window provided a clear view of his neighbor's driveway.

Joe tried to account for Jim driving back to Nassau County, parking the car and then walking home. He wondered what Jim would do if the spot he took Michelle's car from was now occupied. It was a long shot considering the time of day, but it would present a problem.

A short while later he was peering out the window when he saw Jim walk up his driveway and into his home. Joe wondered if he'd share the details of tonight with Sam.

Joe slid into bed with the intention of not waking up his wife. She rolled over but went right back to sleep. He folded his hands on his chest and stared at the ceiling. The detective had to admit that his neighbor had concocted a pretty clever plan. *But why the hell was he doing this?*

If Sam hadn't gotten that ticket, Joe and the Task Force would still be in the dark. Well, actually, except for him, the Task Force *was* still in the dark.

There was one more piece that Joe needed before he could fully and completely put the plan he was formulating into action. That came several hours later. An early morning jogger found a body with a single gunshot wound to the head in an alley next to a burned out OTB in East Elmhurst, Queens. Victim number 16.

Chapter 33

Joe had a lot to think about as he was stuck in traffic on his way the to the 115. He knew Jim Bradley was his man, although everything else surrounding this case was a mystery. The only people he'd allowed to help were his brother-in-law and his old partner, and that was only on a peripheral level. Neither had any hardcore facts and Joe had chosen not to clue either in any further. For his purposes, advising the task force about last night's activities wouldn't be wise and would have to wait. Possibly forever. He was toying around with an idea while shaving, eating breakfast and now in traffic. Some plans sound great on paper, but don't always translate well when put into practice. Joe didn't have long to decide how he wanted to handle the events that transpired the prior evening.

With coffee in hand, he entered his precinct, put his jacket on his chair, and went immediately to the command center. He had a feeling that he wouldn't have to make this trip for much longer. Inspector Ferguson was on the phone at his desk, scribbling madly on a legal pad. Joe figured that either his girlfriend was cracking his walnuts or that the deli had screwed up his breakfast order. It could also have been business, but Joe doubted it, even though Ken had turned out to be a bigger contributor than he had originally imagined. His best contribution, as far as Joe was concerned, was staying the hell out of his way. Joe sat at his desk and sifted through countless e-mails and a voluminous pile of paper. *What to do next?*

He drummed his fingers on his desk, then scrolled through his phone for his neighbor's cell phone number. He had never before called him during working hours and hoped not to spook him.

Jim answered on the second ring. "Hello, this is James Bradley."

Joe figured he hadn't looked down at his phone before answering to see who the caller was.

"Good morning, Counselor. This is Detective Devlin."

"Oh, yes. How are you, Joe?"

"Fine, you?"

"The day just started. I'll let you know in about eight hours."

"Hope I didn't catch you in court."

"No," Jim assured him. "I'll be at my desk for about another half hour before I have to leave. What can I do for you?"

"Well, I'm a little embarrassed, and I guess it could've waited. It's not a big thing. I was just thinking what a nice time we had when we ate at the Leaning Tower. I thought maybe, if you had no other plans, we could do the same tonight?"

"I have no plans tonight," Jim said in a formal and inquisitive tone of voice. "I have a nonexistent social calendar. How about if we meet at the foot of your driveway around 7:30 tonight?"

Joe's mouth curved into a smile. "Sounds good. I'll tell Patty to only prepare dinner for herself."

"Why don't you ask her to join us?"

"I appreciate that, Jim, and you know she loves your company. But she's been a little run down the past few days and told me she wants to get to bed early tonight."

"Okay, as long as she knows she's welcome. Tell her I hope she feels better. See you tonight."

"I'll pass that along, Jim, thanks. See you then."

Joe put his cell phone back in his pocket and looked up to see Ferguson loitering near his desk, briskly rubbing his hands together. He looked like Tom Selleck's character in

Blue Bloods, but without the swagger or brains.

"You look a little flummoxed, Ken, can I help?"

"Sure, Joe, the overnight guys left some documents for my review. Could you give me a second set of eyes to peruse them?"

Joe forced a smile. "Of course." How could he say no? This case could break any day now, or maybe even tonight, not that Ken was aware of that. The two walked together to Ken's desk. For Joe, it was an unnecessary task, as he had his man. Still, not wanting to seem rude to a man who'd never treated him with any kind of disrespect, he obliged Ken's request and started to go over the documents he handed him.

Joe shared his thoughts about the information the overnight guys had dug up. He left out the part about the information being interesting, yet useless. It pointed to a drifter or transient type with a history of drug abuse and mental illness as a possible suspect. In general, this was well-developed evidence and a credible lead. Specific to this case, it was more significant as a liner for a birdcage. However, for Joe, it might prove useful for his needs. Somewhere during his phone conversation with Jim he'd made the decision to see if the plan he'd conceived in his head could be put into effect. There'd be no turning back now.

Chapter 34

Anakin met Jim at the door as usual. Tonight, he seemed to be on overdrive. The rambunctious Rottweiler nearly knocked Jim to the floor. He collected himself, put his briefcase and coat on the couch, and rushed his dog outside.

Anakin came back inside to devour his dinner. His owner mentioned to him that meatballs would be forthcoming a little later in the evening.

Jim was hungry also, but knew he'd be eating at the Leaning Tower, so he grabbed some cashews, almonds and a bottle of water. He headed upstairs for a change of clothes and some light stretching. His train had been delayed as he'd returned home a little later than usual. Now he was rushed to meet his neighbor at 7:30 p.m. Not that Joe would mind waiting a few minutes, but Jim detested being late.

Downstairs, he twisted off the cap of another water bottle, took a big swig, then returned the bottle to the frig. Jim would finish off that bottle following his walk and his meal. Knowing Vincenzo, he would need the water to wash down his antacid.

He stood on his porch taking in the comfortable late April night air. He found his neighbor already in the street, attempting to touch his toes.

"I've always found that it is easier to do that while sitting down, Joe."

"If I could stand up straight right now, I'd hit you."

"Good evening to you as well."

They were now ready for their walk to Vincenzo's. They took the same route as they had a few months prior, almost as if they were on autopilot. But there was an uncomfortable silence as they turned onto Liberty Blvd. from Greene Ave. Jim was surprised at how quiet Joe was, especially since he had taken the time early this morning to extend the invitation. Maybe something was on his mind and he was waiting for the right moment to share it. The only audible sounds were some crickets and a dog off in the distance with an occasional bark.

Jim felt he should break the silence.

"Everything alright, Joe? You seem faraway tonight."

"Yeah, sure. Sorry. Just a lot on my mind. You know how it is."

The men were now picking up a little pace as they reached Pine Ave.

"Speaking of which, how's it going with the investigation?"

"That's exactly what has been preoccupying me, Jim. Very well. I finally caught a break."

Joe's positive declaration stunned Jim. He felt his heartbeat more rapidly and his pulse accelerate. He hadn't read in the papers or seen anywhere online that they were anywhere near solving these murders. "You found your guy?"

"In a manner of speaking," replied Joe with a wry smile.

"Is someone in custody as we speak?"

"No, not yet. My guy doesn't yet know I'm on to him. I'm going to share that tidbit with him at the appropriate time."

Jim was struggling with these cryptic answers. "I'm afraid that I'm not following you, Joe."

"But I've been following you, Jim, that's how this whole thing broke. It's not where it started, but it's where it led me."

Joe's responses were worrying Jim. He began to feel trapped. They walked in silence for a minute as they approached Pine Ave. Jim had to tread lightly now, as he was getting the feeling he sometimes got in court when opposing counsel was about to unveil a biggie. Still, he remained poised. There was no need to appear defensive at this time, especially since he wasn't sure where Joe was heading.

Joe continued, "I like you, Jim, so I'm gonna cut through the bullshit."

"Please do, and I like you as well."

"Under normal circumstances, my usual procedure would be to bring a suspect down to the station and have a little chat with him, or her, and I usually get my guy, or gal. Not with force, although I'm not always against it, but with experience, guile and strong interrogation techniques."

As the two men reached Grove Ave., Jim stopped walking and turned to look Joe squarely in the face. Before he could say anything, the detective beat him to the punch.

"We can continue to walk and talk, Jim."

"Okay," Jim said, feeling jittery.

Both men regained their stride.

"At this point you're probably a little curious about where I'm going with this, and possibly a bit anxious. Please just keep bearing with me."

What other choice did Jim have? His anxiety was rising.

"You see, I know something about you that you probably aren't aware that I know. It puts you in a position of weakness at the moment. I will tell you shortly."

"Really, Joe, you have me stumped. I'm glad that you've made progress with your investigation, but I don't know what any of this has to do with me."

"We're past that now, Counselor, if you'd allow me to continue."

Jim nodded his head in agreement, trying to hide his concern and apprehension. But he could feel his heart rate increasing. He wished he'd ordered dinner from Door Dash.

"I want to tell you a little story, Jim. Stop me if I reach a point where I lose you. Fair enough? Okay. You see, there was a mensch of an accountant, we'll call him Sam, who is so rules-oriented and anxiety riddled that he called up his brother-in-law, who's an NYPD detective, and asked him, actually begged him, to fix a speeding ticket he'd gotten in Corona. This wasn't your ordinary speeding ticket given by a cop, but rather a photograph snapped by one of those Big Brother Red Light Cameras. An image was housed in a database in the Queens Traffic Violations Bureau. Are you with me so far, Jim?"

"I'm still standing. Actually, I'm still walking."

"Good, that's good. Anyway, the brother-in-law, let's call him Joe, felt he owed a lifetime debt to Sam, so he agreed to help out. Joe drove one morning to the Queens Traffic Violations Bureau to carry out the favor, and there he found something very interesting. By a remarkable coincidence, Joe's neighbor, let's call him James, or Jim, had received a speeding ticket from the very same camera a few minutes later. Not damning, of course, but pretty interesting. I haven't lost you, have I Jim?"

Jim's calmness was beginning to erode. His mouth went dry, and he chewed his lips. In a sheepish tone, he assured Joe that he was right with him, although he didn't know what his neighbor's endgame was.

"Over the next several months, the detective took painstaking efforts to put his neighbor under surveillance, hopefully without his pal catching on. He was unsuccessful for quite some time, until he caught a break. Sometimes a little luck is the best plan. It seems that Jim was a regimented walker, rarely detouring from his route. But on this particular night, let's call it last night, Jim did take a detour. Quite a significant one. All the way to the train station parking lot, where he picked up a car. By another remarkable coincidence, it was the same car that Jim had been driving when he got the aforementioned ticket in Corona. The car in question, a gray Honda, was registered to Jim's sister-in-law, let's call her Michelle. The detective observed Jim drive out of the parking lot and onto the westbound LIE. Joe didn't follow him onto the LIE, but our story doesn't end there."

Jim was distressed by the direction in which Joe was

headed. He was particularly disturbed and concerned at his neighbor's mention of Michelle. He fought hard to conceal how bothered he felt.

Joe stopped talking and both men stopped walking as they reached the Leaning Tower of Pizza. As they'd walked and talked, they'd been staring straight ahead. Now they peered into each other's eyes. Joe held the door open for Jim as they entered. Vincenzo greeted his pals, commented on how great it was to see them together again, and showed them to their same table by the window. Jim took a long sip of water while Joe folded his napkin across his lap and continued, without missing a beat.

"Our hero, Joe, and I like to make the cop the hero, placed a call to his ex-partner, let's call him Al, to ask his guys to keep a lookout for a certain gray Honda. Unfortunately, the car wasn't spotted until it was already on the eastbound LIE, after the damage was done. The damage being a 16th victim, which by another coincidence, was found in the area of Queens that Jim had just driven through, and where Jim several months earlier had received a speeding ticket courtesy of modern technology."

Jim felt like he was in court and his adversary was delivering an opening statement. He didn't know all of the evidence Joe had, but the detective had laid a foundation even before the salads were served.

"Don't feel you need to comment, Jim. It is sort of a hypothetical, anyway. We're just two guys talking here."

Jim didn't know much, but he knew that at this moment in time, he and Joe were far more than just two guys talking. He shifted uncomfortably in his chair.

"But taking it a step further," Joe continued, "like I said before, my normal practice would be to bring you in, hypothetically, and interrogate you for hours. Meanwhile, I'd get search warrants, subpoenas, etc. to obtain further evidence if I couldn't get it from the person I was questioning. Chances are I would find little since you, I mean our guy, is highly intelligent and very careful. But if you turn a perps life upside down something usually shakes out, even if this guy isn't your everyday perp. For instance, I'd have to go to a certain sister-in-law and ask her if she knew that her car was the vehicle being used by a killer responsible for 16 deaths, that we know of."

Jim looked up at Joe from his salad, quietly blowing air out of his cheeks. He wasn't sure if Joe had already questioned Michelle, or if she was in custody. If his sister-in-law was sitting in a dark and dingy room in Joe's precinct, had she been told of Jim's role in the murders? The thought of either possibility regarding his sister-in-law alarmed Jim, made him panicky.

"Understand, Jim, I was just giving you an example. We're still in the hypothetical world, for the moment. Frankly, none of this unpleasantness needs to come out. I was hoping that we could help each other. Are you interested?"

Jim swallowed some water and cleared his throat. "Yes, very. He felt a small measure of relief and calmness, and his curiosity was piqued. He let out a slow smile and a huge breath.

"With that as our understanding and agreement, let's move our conversation from the hypothetical to the actual. I mentioned to you how I proceed under normal circumstances. By now, I'm sure you've surmised that I'm not operating in the manner in which I usually do. That is by design, Jim. Since I trust your word, I'm going to share something that I've never revealed to anyone, except of course my wife."

Jim moved back from the table to allow Vincenzo to place his dish down in front of him. He was hanging on every word, vacillating between fear and fascination.

Joe pressed on. "As you know, my son, Thomas, was killed a few years ago. Since then, Patty and I have been going through the motions, each in our own way. Patty has retreated away from society and become virtually housebound. She's bordering on agoraphobic. It's killing me to watch her emotionally deteriorate. As for me, I now find police work, at one time my life's passion, to be at best mundane and at worst intolerable. Sadness and depression are forming such a dark cloud over us. I feel we'll never get out from under it."

"Several weeks ago, a former cop called me up right out of the blue. We'd worked together years back at the 110. We were never partners but had a good rapport. Anyway, he's moved out to San Diego and now runs a firm that specializes in security work. He offered me a position right on the phone. I'm up to my eyeballs with this serial killer thing, so I tell him I need time to think about it. But now as this thing is close to wrapping up, I think it would be a good thing for Patty and me. A change of scenery, a different coast, great weather. I'd retire with honor from the NYPD, take my pension with me, work in the private sector and start a new life. What do you think?"

Jim didn't know what to think. He felt that Joe had been forthcoming but had left out a few key parts. "It's a good plan, Joe, and I'm sure it's for the best. I wish you and Patty all the luck. Can I ask you a few questions?"

"Let me stop you there, Jim. I feel I've been dominating the evening and I'm sick of the sound of my own voice. However, it would be best if I asked you a few questions. Remember, Jim, everything said at this table is in the spirit of our agreement and understanding that we will ultimately help each other. Am I clear?"

"Crystal, Joe."

"Excellent. Let's start with this. When I finally caught the guy, and at times during this investigation I wasn't always sure I would, if he was lucid and rational and not a deranged fruitcake, I promised myself I'd ask him how he could manage to commit such atrocities and stay remotely sane and normal?"

Jim pressed his lips together, and his jaw clenched.

"You can speak freely, Jim, I assure you. Remember, just two guys talking. If it would make you feel more at ease, respond in the hypothetical. But I'm very interested."

Jim sat back and wiped his hands with his napkin. He had to seriously consider what he said and how he said it. "Okay, Joe. I'd think he'd plan everything very precisely, choosing victims he's not connected to. It might be completely random, as you've told me several times involving this case. The victims might be on the fringes of society, drug addicts and sex sellers. Those whose disappearance wouldn't lead the evening news. He might see these individuals as a means to an end. He might even perceive his prey as not just as a means to an end, but worthy of only extreme contempt."

"The guy probably chooses places where the victims aren't expecting it, where they'd be surprised. His escape route would be meticulously mapped out, and he's fully prepared to delay action any time he encounters unforeseen circumstances."

"That fascinates me, Jim. So, tell me this. Why does the serial killer hold such an extreme and irrational disregard for others? I mean, how can he build up such hate, anger and resentment toward an individual whom he's never met?"

Jim's eyes wandered up, then met Joe's. "It's difficult to say for certain. I would imagine that, quite possibly, your guy might have had some extremely deep-rooted anger built up under the surface. Hatred he unsuccessfully tried to extinguish in therapy. He might be the type of guy who kept everything all bottled up. Then one day, he encountered tragedy, the cap was twisted off, and all the bad stuff that was dormant seeped out and reared its ugly head.

"Your guy could be the type that looked like a winner but felt like a loser. You know the type, Detective. He looks all together but actually is falling apart. Disappointments personally and professionally that build hostility and resentment. A tedious life that morphs into dissatisfaction at best, hatred at worst. But that's just a theory."

"Yes, I understand completely. Another thing. Many of the perps I have collared got sloppy at the crime scene, but this guy left us nothing, even with 16 victims. How can you explain that?"

"As you know, Detective, your guy is motivated differently than a typical criminal. Someone walking or driving in the area, a loud noise, whatever, would scare him away. He's patient and deliberate, rather that rushed and haphazard. He's very careful and exact. Again, he selects remote spots hoping to find derelicts, drifters, transients, drug users and sex workers, assuming that they might not have a large contingent wondering where they are or what happened to them. In addition, if it was a drifter or drug-addict type that killed his brother, bitterness might have built up against them. I'm just going by what I have read and heard on the subject."

Vincenzo came around to clear the table and offer coffee and dessert. Since they were sure their conversation required more time, both accepted Vin's offer. Coffee and cheesecake for the detective, coffee and cannolis for the counselor. Vin responded with a "very good" and hustled away. Jim took this opportunity to visit the men's room, while Joe went outside to fill his lungs with some night air and tobacco.

Several minutes later, both returned to their table like boxers returning to the middle of the ring following a between rounds respite. Joe commented on how good the meal was, and Jim agreed. Vincenzo brought over the coffee and dessert, and the men eyed their sweets as masters would eye their chess pieces. Both were ready for the game to continue, but neither knew who would make the next move.

Chapter 35

Joe put a fork into his cheesecake and decided he'd be the one to break the awkward silence. "I appreciate your thoughts in trying to help me understand this serial killer. We've been going back and forth for a while now, talking in circles and pussyfooting around. As our meal is drawing to a close, I suggest we get down to the business at hand."

Jim wiped at a small dab of cannoli cream that remained on the corner of his mouth. "You've lost me a bit, Joe. What did you have in mind?"

"Right. Let's get to that. The smart thing for me to do would be to bring you in."

The coffee Jim was sipping ended up adorning the front of his shirt. He dipped a napkin into his water and rubbed at the stain vigorously.

"Sorry. You see I've shifted from the hypothetical to the actual, just to make it more interesting. I should bring you in and break you, legally of course, and then retire on top. My superiors would give me the hero treatment and would be happy to accept my retirement and assist in my transition to our new life in San Diego."

"Not that I want you to follow that plan, but is something keeping you from it?" Jim asked.

Joe observed Jim deftly blotting beads of sweat that were forming on his forehead and upper lip.

"Unfortunately, yes. I have developed an alternate plan I believe to be mutually beneficial. Are you interested?"

"Since I have no appetite for plan A, I'm fine with hearing plan B."

"I'm somewhat embarrassed to tell you that solving these

murders is no longer my motivation. You suffered a great loss also Jim, maybe you'll understand. Since I lost my son, I have slowly become more and more despondent, increasingly unable to cope with life's daily grind. My bitterness and vitriol have eroded my sense of humanity, to a large degree. Don't misunderstand, I feel deeply for these victims and their families. Their faces are all up on the wall in my command center, and I hurt for each one. But like I said, my family has been shattered. Patty is rapidly declining, withdrawing from life. It's an ethical conundrum, I admit that."

"I can't say I can blame you for feeling that way, Joe. Lord knows since my brother's death I've never been the same. I'm getting worse each day. But I'm not sure where I fit into this."

The detective leaned in and met the counselor's eyes. "Before I get into that, I need a few things explained. I'm going to ask you to be a little forthcoming, and it'll require some trust on your part. We're still operating under the bond of our agreement to help each other."

"Go ahead, Joe, shoot."

"On the surface, you're the All-American boy. Good looking, athletic, career, nice car, nice house, the works. But obviously something isn't as it appears. I need to know why a successful attorney turned into a monthly killing machine."

"That's a loaded question, Joe."

"It is better than facing a loaded gun."

"I can't argue with that. Okay, good question. A while back in the evening you told me a story. I'd like to reciprocate and tell you one."

"I'm all ears, Counselor."

"Several years ago, a bright, energetic and kind man, let's call him David, was working at his Queens office late one night. He loved his wife, let's call her Michelle, very much. They hadn't been blessed with children yet, but desperately wanted them. On that night he went to the parking lot behind his building to get to his car when he was stopped by an individual with a gun who demanded money. Instead of David just giving it up, he struggled with this man and was killed. A gunshot to the heart. His death was instantaneous. We later learned that his killer, let's call him Henry Vernon, was a deranged drug addict with a rap sheet longer than the Nile River."

Joe closed his eyes to signify his emotional understanding of the pain this must have caused the Bradley family.

Jim continued on in a trance-like state. "To add insult to injury, this man was never brought to justice. A sloppy investigation by some incompetent Queens cops, coupled with an even greater level of ineptness on the part of the Queens District Attorney's office, lead to the charges being dropped and this animal being let back out on the streets."

"So then about six years go by, and then what?"

"Then the older brother, let's call him Jim, sees his parents deteriorate, just as you described has been happening to your wife. He witnesses devastating pain emanating from them, as well as from his sister-in-law. As the years go by, Jim's anger and bitterness fester uncontrollably. Not only was David taken from them, but Vernon never had to answer for his crime. There's no release for Jim's pain. Ultimately, after months of stewing over an idea, his visceral instincts overcome him and he searches for and kills Henry Vernon, near the spot Vernon had killed his brother. If you review your list of victims, you'll see that the first one is named Henry Vernon, killed with a single gunshot to the heart, even though he didn't have one."

Joe had mixed feelings about the yarn his friend had spun. He stared at his dessert, massaging his temples, then stroked his chin. "That's an intriguing tale. But where would a buttoned-down Manhattan attorney obtain a semi-automatic pistol, an M1911, and how would this attorney become such a good shot?"

"In keeping with the actual, a childhood friend, who now resides in Paris, was from a family of gun nuts. He taught all the Bradley men how to shoot. We're all accurate shooters. The gun in question was obtained somewhat illegally following David's murder. A former client of mine set up a meeting for me. I cut through the red tape and registering hassle."

"Up to this point, Jim, I'm with you. Getting the gun, killing Vernon, I get it. But 15 people were killed following Vernon. That's where you lose me."

"Killing that scum was pleasing, but not enough to eradicate the pain. My anger started to spin out of control, and my hatred towards Queens, its cops, District Attorneys and citizens knew no limits. I sought out counseling but settled on revenge."

"I lost my faith. That's when it all started, and once it did, I couldn't stop. Finally, I didn't want to. So, I did my own thing, and you know what, in the end, it got done."

"You see Joe, it started out being about revenge and anger, but then it became more about the rush I got and the relief I felt. The sense of power and control. These were the only times since David's murder that I felt that way."

Joe noticed that Jim was speaking more quickly and sweat trickled in steams down his face. The detective had heard enough confessions to know not to interrupt when the suspect was unburdening himself.

"I sought out committing crimes that would be unsolvable. No motive and no connection to or between the victims. Henry Vernon was the only one targeted. The rest were random drug addicts, prostitutes and homeless. My goal was to humiliate and embarrass the police and the DA, and to force the public to squeeze the crap out of both."

"On that last point your plan was a success."

"I had selfishly hoped to soothe my soul, but on that point my plan wasn't a success. It just made me more desensitized and the victims more dehumanized."

"One thing, Jim, your sister-in-law, Michelle, is she in on it? Does she know what's going on?"

Jim bulled his neck and in a slow and meaningful tone responded, "She's not aware of any of this. I'm sorry she got dragged in. Michelle has suffered greatly and anything to do with her is off the table. That's not negotiable."

Not wishing for their meeting to travel down this path, Joe assured Jim that he had no interest in being punitive toward Michelle. "I was just curious, Jim. Call it a cop's intrigue. But I'll get off the subject as it serves neither of our purposes."

"Fine, Joe. Thanks."

Joe saw Vincenzo coming with the check and his standard two York Peppermint patties, plus Anakin's order. He felt compelled to speak. "I appreciate your candor, Jim, and your trust. I feel I owe you the same in return. The reason that I didn't just follow protocol and go through police channels on this one is that I still have extreme pain and distress, and hopefully you can provide a cure for that."

Jim's face went blank.

"You see, Jim, you never asked me how my son was killed, and I never volunteered it. Thomas was going to be late getting home one night after baseball practice, so he took a short cut through a wooded area near Sanders Parkway. As he was coming out of the woods behind Bailey's Auto Repair Shop, a drugged-out lunatic jumped him. A struggle ensued, and he was stabbed to death."

Joe looked down at the goose pimples that had formed on his arms just re-telling that story. He showed Jim, who grimaced and ran his hand through his hair.

"Now, I'm a cop, a detective no less, so you should figure that this is a no-brainer. But some jerk-off Nassau County cops screwed up. The investigation gets botched, some evidence is obtained illegally, and the whole thing gets thrown out. Patty and I are left with unbearable heartbreak and no closure, just like your family. Some cop buddies of mine try to find this bastard, but he disappears from the area. However, a little while back, a Nassau County detective calls me up to let me know that the guy who killed my son, Keith Jenkins, was spotted in the area. They brought him in on a drug sweep, but they put him back on the streets. Nine lives this prick's got."

Joe had a way of stopping right when Jim was most interested. Jim sighed, unwrapped a piece of candy and aggressively polished off his coffee.

They split the check again, said goodnight and thanks to Vincenzo, and left the restaurant. The men had only been outside for a moment when Joe turned to Jim and said, "This is where you come into my plan."

"What would you like me to do?"

"Balance the books, similar to the way you made Henry Vernon accountable for what he did to your brother."

Joe stopped walking and looked Jim squarely in the eyes. The men were standing about five feet apart. Joe realized that his life would be forever and irreversibly changed based upon the next few moments. He wondered if Jim was thinking the same thing.

Joe said, "Henry Vernon got what he deserved, what was just. I'd like Keith Jenkins to experience the same fate. I'll speak your language. Think of it as an oral contract, Counselor. I'm willing to destroy any and all evidence and information gathered by me, which would give someone the impression that you were the "Period Killer." I can assure you that the Task Force Team has not been privy to my investigation of you. In return, you'll do me the favor of killing the man who murdered our son and our soul. I've recently collected some data and material regarding the whereabouts and the comings and goings of Keith Jenkins. Do we have a deal, Counselor?"

"How would this work, Joe? The mechanics of it, I mean. And don't you want to be the one who closes this case?"

"Always an attorney, Jim, I admire that. I *will* be closing this case. Right now, I have a file on my desk that Inspector Ferguson shared with me. Some of the men on my team like this guy for the murders. He's a drifter, a transient, with major drug issues and a history of violence and mental health issues. Brian Paige was dishonorably discharged from the Army. He spends a lot of time in the general area of where many of the murders occurred. Also, Paige is extremely ill as a result of years of I.V. drug use, along with other self-destructive behavior. Apparently, he doesn't have much time left."

They began to walk again, at a slow and plodding pace.

"This is a good thing for Patty and me," Joe said. "She's my whole world right now. We'll need a few months to handle our affairs and tie up some loose ends. By October we hope to be in San Diego. I was hoping that prior to our departure our plan could be put into action. This way we could start fresh in California, with no unfinished business here in New York.

"Oh, and by the way, Jim, it's my understanding that your firm has a San Francisco office. I suggest you look into transferring there afterward. You seem to be stagnating here, and it'll provide an opportunity for you to put the past behind you as well. Who knows, with us all out of the left coast, maybe we could share another holiday together? And I assume that no serial killer will appear in California, say in the Bay area?"

"You've really thought this scheme through, Detective. It's not exactly what I dreamed of when I was in moot court back in law school, but okay, I like your idea. About the San Francisco office I mean. Sound advice. I've been running in place for years. A move like that will be the shot in the arm I need. And you have my word that there will be no other shots."

"That's good to hear, Counselor. But what about..?"

Jim interrupted Joe in mid-sentence. "Regarding that other matter we discussed. I can make that work. I'm happy to help. You shouldn't give that another minute's worry."

They had reached Forest Ave. and Joe's house. Joe

extended his hand, which Jim shook. "Thank you, Jim. It was nice doing business with you."

Jim flashed a smile. "Likewise. Just one more thing. To reiterate, all communication tonight is covered by attorney-cop privilege, isn't that correct, Detective?"

"It is, Counselor. As soon as you're able to fulfill your end of the arrangement, I will hold up my end. You have my word. As far as I am concerned, this case has been closed."

"Good, Joe. Have a good night and don't let this weigh on you anymore."

"Same to you, neighbor."

Chapter 36

The day following his long, yet worthwhile evening spent with Jim Bradley, Joe brought in Brian Paige for questioning. In the room with him during the interrogation were Russell Hollander and Kenneth Ferguson. Brenner and Captain Sterling observed the proceedings from the other side of the glass.

They spent many laborious hours going over every detail and piece of minutia. Paige had been surprisingly lucid for the first few hours but was beginning to show signs of wear and tear as the day dragged into the evening - just as Joe had counted on. The detective knew two things. First, Paige was a career drug addict and soon would need a major fix. Second, in his compromised medical condition, he might own up to the murders just to cease this endless question and answer period. He wasn't certain if the suspect would lawyer up, which would present some challenging new variables.

Satisfied that they had gotten all that they could've gotten from Paige that day, he was released, but told not to plan any trips. The suspect wearily stumbled out of the command center and the precinct, undoubtedly on his way to a long night of guzzling booze and injecting needles.

Joe had suggested to Ferguson that they keep Paige under surveillance. Ken told him it was already in the works. "I think Paige is our guy, but we're weak on evidence. We'll need a search warrant for his place."

Joe knew Paige lived in a real dump and was a very on-again off-again car mechanic. His daily drug use had cost him many jobs, and now he was again between jobs. He was one step away from being homeless again. Robbing and stealing to support his habit had become a lifestyle.

Hollander came over to where Joe and Ferguson were sitting and interrupted their conversation. He was tapping away at his cell phone, then his steely eyes met Joe's. "I don't want to throw cold water on this legitimate suspect, but I don't think he's our guy. Some things fit, but most don't. He doesn't really fit the profile, based on my experience. We should keep an eye on him, no doubt, but I don't know. I want the guy as bad as you do, but we have to be certain he's the right one."

Joe had expected Hollander not to be sold. Based on his resume and Joe's experience with him, he was about as sharp as it got in terms of this type of case.

"I have the same concern, Russ, believe me. That's why we cut him loose. We really can't hold him, but I wanted to throw a scare into him. We'll watch him and monitor his activities. Unfortunately, right now he's all we have and we're not in a position to dismiss anyone.

"We'll search his apartment and try to speak with someone from his last job. I'll also talk with the people who ran the last homeless shelter he flopped at. Maybe we'll get lucky, and something will turn up."

Ferguson left the meeting, advising Joe that he planned to round up the team for a briefing about these latest developments. Hollander was scheduled to be on a plane to Washington D.C. later in the day. "I hope to be back in a week, Joe. Two at the latest. But I'll be available by cell, so please don't hesitate to contact me if anything breaks."

"Absolutely, Russ. Have a good trip."

"Thanks, Joe. Good luck with Mr. Paige."

With Ferguson engaged in capacity planning and budgetary concerns and Hollander headed for the nation's capital, Joe had a little elbowroom. He planned to get a search warrant and execute it at Paige's apartment but didn't anticipate finding anything helpful. Planting evidence was not an option. He really didn't have any, except for what he had collected on Jim Bradley, which was headed for a barrel of hydrochloric acid once Part A of his plan was completed. Even the search warrant was no slam-dunk given their evidence. They were weak on probable cause.

Joe considered calling Jim Bradley and taking him up on his offer of assistance in obtaining a warrant but decided against it. Joe didn't want to push it after the two had struck a compromise the previous evening. He walked over to Brenner, who was chewing the fat with Sterling and the Inspector. Joe asked Harry if he could facilitate obtaining permission to a search warrant; of course, Brenner agreed, not wanting the commissioner to have his posterior for Sunday brunch.

Joe persuaded Ferguson to allow him to embark on a solo mission to Paige's apartment, citing manpower issues and busy phones. Ferguson wanted to send someone to tag along but relented. The detective left the 115 to see the judge who issued the warrant, then he'd head to the suspect's apartment. The noise Joe heard in his head was the sound of the case closing. Hopefully.

Joe always confessed to his wife that sometimes a little luck was the best plan. In fact, it was some good fortune that helped him identify his neighbor as the killer.

While searching Brian Paige's filthy apartment, he couldn't believe what he came across. Underneath a pile of dirty magazines and even dirtier clothes was a wallet. Joe had his latex gloves on, and he reached down for it. The cash and credit cards had been removed, but the rest of the items hadn't been disturbed. It had belonged to Nicholas Graham, the 16th victim, killed a few days ago.

But how did Paige obtain this? No wallet had been found on the victim. He was identified after Joe's team had found a dry-cleaning ticket in the pocket of Nicholas Graham's windbreaker. Devlin could only assume that since Paige lived in the area where the body was found, he must've been wandering around trying to score drugs and discovered

Graham's dead body. Paige must have removed the wallet and fled the scene. *What a break*! He spent a few more minutes looking around, then left Paige's apartment, with Graham's wallet in an evidence bag.

Joe tailed it back to the precinct, anxious to wrap this up and get on with his life. Ferguson was on yet another one of his "important" phone calls. Joe gestured to him that he had an urgent matter to discuss. While he waited for Ken to finish his dinner order, Joe texted Hollander and provided a full report. Hollander obviously was involved in something critical at the time, so his response was simply a "thumbs up."

When Ken came over, Joe shared his new piece of evidence and informed him that he'd already arranged for Brian Paige to be picked up. "Excellent work, Detective," Ferguson said. "I'll call Harry. He'll want to be here when we interrogate the suspect. Again, great job, Joe."

"Thanks, Ken. I already told Russ. I'll advise Lt. Moss and Captain Sterling. Harry will probably want to contact the commissioner."

The accused was brought to the command center in handcuffs about thirty minutes later. Joe surmised that Mr. Paige had kept to his usual diet of heroin, pills and liquor. Joe further theorized that Paige was in better condition than he would've been if they'd waited until the wee hours of the night.

Brian Paige was in his forties, with pale, sickly skin. He had thinning black hair and was wearing a Grateful Dead t-shirt and extremely faded, formerly blue, jeans. His health was failing rapidly. Joe had his medical records and learned that Paige had contracted Hepatitis B several years ago and was now living with a failing liver. For the second time that day, he was brought into the interrogation room in the command center. On the way into the room, Ferguson asked Joe to handle the interview. *Was there another option?*

Joe took his position to the left of Paige, Ferguson to the

right. Brenner was in his usual spot, unseen behind the partition. Captain Sterling had been dispatched to One PP by the commissioner, so Brenner was in the observation room with only Borough Detective Amanda Gordon.

"Would you like a cigarette, Mr. Paige?" Joe asked.

"Yes, I would."

Joe reached into the breast pocket of his shirt and extended him a Marlboro, which he gratefully accepted. Joe lit the cigarette.

"Things are very much different now than they were earlier today, Brian. We have some issues that need clarity. Maybe you can help us straighten some of these things out. Let's start with this." Joe took the wallet that belonged to Nicholas Graham from his pants pocket and placed it on the desk in front the suspect.

Paige, who already looked feeble and fatigued, put his head in his hands, then directed his gaze toward Joe. He went on to explain that he had stumbled across the body as he was out walking after midnight. "Ok, ok, I was on my way to meet a guy to score drugs. I admit that. I took the guy's wallet, yes. I know it was wrong, but I'm really sick. These drugs help me get through the day. But I promise you guys, I had nothing to do with killing that guy. He was already dead when I found him."

This back and forth went on for some hours. At one point, Joe stared closely into Paige's eyes for effect, and noticed that they were jaundiced. The suspect was losing his strength and his will with each passing minute. He then asked for some medical attention due to severe abdominal pain. Joe, assuming it was a stalling technique, told him soon, but not now.

Paige complained of nausea and said he had to throw up. Joe opened the door and yelled for Det. Lempert, who he asked to accompany Mr. Paige to the bathroom.

Upon returning, Lempert reported to Joe that Paige had indeed vomited and was truly in discomfort. Paige gingerly walked back into the room. He was slouched over in a "C" curve, alternating placing one hand on his lower back and one on his stomach. Joe thought he looked ten years older than he had that same morning.

The Detective was about to tell Paige that he was calling for medical aid when the suspect slumped out of his chair and slid onto the floor. Joe rushed to help him up and put him back in his chair but could see Paige was struggling. He turned to Ferguson and asked him to get Dr. Evans down the street and bring him back for treatment.

As soon as Ferguson left the room, Paige collapsed to the floor and passed out. Joe felt for a pulse, which was faint, then called 9-1-1. An ambulance immediately showed up and transported Paige to New York-Presbyterian Hospital, a Level 1 trauma center in Elmhurst.

Joe rode in the ambulance with Paige, who had woken up, but was sweating profusely. His face was colorless. He screamed for pain medicine, then coughed up a phlegm tapestry. Paige muttered a few words to the detective, maybe a confession, maybe a question, maybe a "screw you." Joe couldn't understand what he said. A minute later Brian Paige passed away. One block from the hospital.

Upon arrival, Joe told the awaiting medical personnel that the suspect had died. He turned to Brenner and Ferguson who'd just arrived, racing from their cars to join him. Joe announced that Paige had regained consciousness for just a minute or two, to confess his crimes and clear his conscience.

Chapter 37

Over the next five months, Joe's life became very hectic. Many things had transpired since that April day when Brian Paige died in the ambulance. He had a lot of loose ends to tie up prior to his move to San Diego.

The day following the closing of the case, Commissioner Fields, with Mayor Simpson, Councilman Ortiz and Borough President Buckner at his side, held a press conference to formally announce that the case had been solved, and the perpetrator had died of complications from liver failure. The row behind the commissioner included Chief of Detectives Brenner, Borough Detective Gordon, Inspector Ferguson, Captain Sterling, Lt. Moss and Detective Devlin.

Commissioner Fields was effusive in his praise of the tremendous efforts of the Task Force Team, along with FBI Agent Russell Hollander, citing their round the clock work, diligence and commitment to keep New York City safe. He also held a moment of silence to remember Paige's 16 victims. Fields turned the microphone over to the elected officials, the police brass and finally to Joe. The detective was very complimentary about how the task force members, regardless of rank or precinct, acted as a team for the purpose of catching the killer. Joe fielded the most questions and was the most candid in his responses. Except for the "Big Truth," about which he wasn't in a position to be candid.

Two days after the press conference, he went to Brenner to inform his boss he was putting in his retirement papers. Brenner was still glowing in the after-effects of the serial killer case getting off the front page, so he was more than happy to grant Joe's request. It really wasn't a request, but out of respect for the kind of cop and individual Harry was, Joe felt it the best approach.

"It's time, Harry. I will always love the NYPD, but it's over now."

"You deserve it, Joe. You've had a great career, but it's probably a good time for Patty and you to start over somewhere else. Take some time. Enjoy the sun and your life. I may be right behind you with my papers."

"Good for you. Give it serious thought. Your career has been exemplary. But now's a good time for Gloria and you to spend some time together, concentrate on good things, like grandchildren."

Harry frowned. "Thanks Joe. I'm so very sorry about your son. I hope you and Patty can find some peace."

"We're going to try. I have a friend whose helping us with that."

"Glad to hear it. I'll miss working with you. I wish you all the best."

"Same here. Be well always."

Joe hadn't gone through the normal channels regarding putting in his papers. But since Brenner was gushing in his heartfelt praise for Joe's tireless work, he felt comfortable going to his boss directly. The only thing Brenner requested was that Lieutenant Moss and Captain Sterling were advised of his plans by the end of the day. Of course, Joe obliged.

Two weeks later, Joe was the recipient of a wonderful retirement party which Brenner orchestrated. He surmised that Brenner's wife had done the nuts and bolts planning, but why should he quibble? They'd rented out a top steakhouse and the night was filled with thank-yous, good-byes, tears, war stories, laughs, great food and great booze. He'd received some terrific gifts, including a beautiful Movado watch and Mount Blanc pen with "Detective Joe Devlin" inscribed on it. Joe had spent the last 28 years of his life with the NYPD, and Brenner clearly wanted this night to be an expression of their gratitude for his years of service.

At the party, Patty Devlin told her sister Elizabeth and brother-in-law Sam how wonderful this night had been. "He deserves his day in the sun. So much of our last few years were set in darkness." Tears formed in the corners of her eyes.

Joe proudly introduced his wife to everyone, as he did Sam and Elizabeth Weiss. Although the night belonged to Joe, it was bittersweet on many levels. All of the reminiscing left him a little sad to leave the NYPD, especially given manner in which his time there had concluded. His decision would keep him up nights, for sure, but he hoped it was the best thing for Patty and him. Joe felt it was the only way to begin to soothe their pain and suffering. They were drowning, and his expectation was that the option he chose would be their life raft. But there was still a moral man down deep inside the detective, and he knew that some decisions could be very hard to live with.

The following weekend, Joe had asked Sam and Elizabeth if they had any interest in moving out to San Diego with them. Sam was pushing 60, and he was set financially. Elizabeth loved the warm weather and hated the idea of her baby sister on the other side of the country. The Weisses told the Devlins they would seriously consider it, in fact were leaning toward doing it. Sam explained that he'd need some time to extricate himself from some partnership duties and responsibilities, but he most likely could make it happen by next spring. Joe and Patty were pleased and told Sam and Elizabeth that they'd start looking for a house for them when they arrived in San Diego in late September or October.

The last loose end that needed tying up was Al Silvani. Joe had explained to Sam why Bradley was not their guy, and he wanted to tell Al the same thing. His former partner had called him immediately after he heard about Brian Paige. They spoke for only a few minutes because Al wasn't feeling that well. Al would have loved to attend the retirement party, but his poor health wouldn't permit it.

Joe called Al again just before the 4th of July, hoping his friend was feeling better.

"Hi Joey, how's the big man on campus?"

"Fine, Al, you sound much better."

"Just a bad flu bug, but I knocked it out. I never got to ask you, with all the excitement of the case being solved, whatever happened with the guy you called me about that night, the car in Corona?"

"It was a false alarm, Al. Wrong guy. Some things weren't adding up, but it all checked out. By the way, I never got a chance to tell you, I put in my papers. I'll be done at the end of the summer and in San Diego by late September or October. I'll be doing some security work at a firm owned by an ex-cop. I was wondering if you have any interest in moving out there? The weather's great."

"It's tempting, Joe. With my wife gone, my time is my own, and the pension takes care of a lot. But my daughter, son-in-law and grandkids are here. They've been great to me. I think I'll stay here for now. But you can count on a visit or two."

"You've got a deal. But keep it in your mind as an option."

"You bet."

"Listen, Al, I know you don't go for mushy, and I'll be around to see you before I leave, but thanks for everything. Your caring and friendship. Your life lessons and job tips. I could never express my appreciation enough that they partnered me with a cop and a person like you."

There was a pause at the other end. Joe knew Al was getting choked up but would never admit it. "The feeling is mutual," Al said, in a low, scratchy voice. "Call me soon and we'll get together and get something to eat. Your treat."

"Okay, soon, have a good 4th."

"Take care always, Joseph."

Joe loved Al, as he did Sam. These are the only two people in the world Joe had trusted with even a small piece of his investigation into Jim Bradley. Neither man pressed him on

Bradley, especially since Brian Paige had been identified as the murderer. Joe felt pangs of guilt that he betrayed the trust of these two great men. He was disappointed in himself but knew this was his only choice to achieve some measure of peace and make a break from the past.

The only individual that wasn't completely sold on Brian Paige being the killer was Russell Hollander, who was needed in Washington DC for longer than expected. The FBI Agent missed the press conference and Joe's retirement party.

Russell had called Joe from DC the first week of June to congratulate him.

"Sorry I couldn't be there at the end, Joe. You know how it goes sometimes. We all have to do our part from time to time and go where we're told. I wanted to tell you how great it was working with you. You're a real pro."

"Thank you, Russell, and no apology necessary. I understand full well. I enjoyed the experience also, and I learned a lot from you. You really know your stuff."

"It would appear that in this instance you knew your stuff. Your instincts told you Paige was the guy, mine didn't. Some of his actions fly in the face of what I've learned and my past experiences. But like I told you before, all cases are different. Not every case fit into a pattern. I of course was pleased to hear that Paige had confessed to you in the ambulance just prior to his death. Kudos to you for making it happen."

"Making it happen" could be taken two ways. It could certainly be concluded that Joe's investigatory skills made the arrest of Paige happen. But Joe knew that he'd literally made the entire pursuit of Paige happen, aware he was the wrong guy. Hollander was among the sharpest people he'd ever been around. He may've had some suspicions that all wasn't as it appeared, but Joe figured that Hollander had calculated that no good would come from cracking open this nut. The right people were happy and satisfied, so logic would dictate filing this one away. Besides, what evidence did Hollander have to go to anyone with a different story? A suspicion was far from proof. Still, Joe knew that if Hollander did suspect something, this would be his clever way of letting him know that the wool couldn't easily be pulled over his eyes.

"I couldn't have closed this case without the lessons you taught me about investigating serial killers. So, we share the credit and go on with our lives. I wish you the best in your future endeavors with the FBI."

"I wish you all the luck as well, Detective. I understand you'll be retiring and moving to San Diego. Great city. Hope you can live with your decision, to move to California I mean, of course."

Joe felt an uptick in his anxiety. He rubbed his forehead between his thumb and middle finger.

"I hope so, too, Russ. We're going to go there with an open mind, closing the door to the past."

In early October, Joe was awoken from a Saturday afternoon nap by a buzzing on the coffee table. The phone slipped from his hand onto the living room rug where Joe reached to retrieved it. He managed an unenthusiastic "Hello."

"Hi, Detective, this is Jim Bradley."

"Long time, no see, Counselor."

"It's been hectic. Between work and going down to Florida to visit my parents, I haven't been around much. How's retirement treating you?"

"Good, so far, Jim. But hectic as well. We've sold the house and went west a couple of times. We finally found a great condo. Patty and I have been busy getting ready to leave. We should be out of here Halloween week. That reminds me. You and I haven't spoken since your Labor Day BBQ. I was hoping we could get a chance to speak soon."

"You read my mind, Joe. I was thinking later tonight we could get together."

"Sounds good. Shall we say 7:00 p.m.? Same meeting

spot."

"I'll be there. Except this time let's skip the Leaning Tower. I've been putting on weight."

"Agreed. Besides, I want you in tip-top shape. Sharp and alert."

"I hate long good-byes, Counselor," Joe said as they accelerated onto Greene Ave. from Forest Ave., "so I thought it a good idea to wish you all the best now."

"You, too, Detective. Please give Patty my best. She's a wonderful lady, especially putting up with you. I wish both of you happiness and peace in your new life."

"That's appreciated. On that subject, I'm expecting that the first part of our agreement will be executed, no pun intended, shortly. That was the gist of our conversation in your backyard on Labor Day. Just to refresh your memory, there were some issues that cropped up in the late summer that disrupted our plan. Thankfully, all logistical and other administrative issues have been resolved, leaving us ready to effectuate the agreed upon proposal."

Joe noticed that Jim was walking more quickly. His breathing was more rapid and small beads of sweat began forming on his upper lip. He brushed at them with his shirt sleeve. "Without getting into much detail, I would keep my ears open around Columbus Day Week. You may hear something you like. There may just be some news that intrigues you."

"That would be great." Joe said. "It would be great for Patty and me to be able to start our new life without looking back. In fact, I'd be so grateful that certain documents, photos and other investigatory material, which is creating a lot of clutter, would be destroyed."

"The entire file, or might an item be kept for posterity?" Jim asked half-jokingly.

"Believe me, Patty and I both desire a clean break from the past. We have no interest in anything that occurred prior to when we land on the West Coast. We'll keep our son and his memory with us forever, but that's the only piece of New York we wish to carry with us."

"Fair enough and understood."

They decided to cut their walk short and head back to their homes. Upon arrival at his house, he and Jim faced each other. Joe was contemplating how their lives had become so intertwined in such a short period of time.

"Jim, I enjoyed meeting you and your family, and am sorry for your loss."

Jim extended his hand, which Joe firmly shook. "Thank you. I feel the same. Very mixed emotions, but glad I got to meet you and Patty. I'm sorry for your loss as well."

"We've both suffered greatly and caused great suffering. Big mistakes were made on our part, and now we have to live with them, although at times it may be difficult. Very difficult."

"At night I have trouble sleeping," Jim confessed. "I can't change the past, or even understand it. It just got out of control. But, as agreed, that part of my life is over. After a quick trip to see my parents, I'm on my way to San Francisco to start a new life as well. I'll be there after the first of the year."

"Good for you, and please give your parents our best."

"This thing could have gone a lot of different ways."

"Yes, it could have indeed," Joe agreed. "But we couldn't have brought the victims back. Brian Paige is no longer with us, and I'm confident that you're now out of business. Hopefully, the families got some measure of closure, as I wish for us."

"On that subject, I'd anticipate that you'll be hearing shortly from the Nassau County police regarding the demise of Keith Jenkins."

Joe flashed a knowing and satisfied smile. "Good night, Counselor. Maybe we'll meet up again one day in California. I wish you luck. Take care."

"Good night, Detective. I look forward to that. I wish you peace."

Following one last handshake, the men strolled up their driveways and disappeared into their homes.

Chapter 38

Jim Bradley arrived home from work a little earlier than usual. It was a short work week, with the Columbus Day holiday creating a three-day respite the prior weekend. Jim had worked long hours Tuesday through Thursday, so he ducked out a little early on Friday. He wished William Dunn a good weekend on his way out but didn't hang around to find Douglas White. There was a better chance of winning Lotto nine weeks in a row than spotting "Old Man" White in the office after 3:00 p.m. on a Friday. Jim understood White's dilemma. How could the senior partner be expected to get to Happy Hour at Donovan's at a reasonable time if he was bogged down with legal work?

In the immediate aftermath of the serial killer case being "solved," both William Dunn and Raymond from *Coffee to Go* had tracked Jim down to discuss the resolution of the police matter with him. Like many people, Dunn and Ray were fascinated with the subject of serial killers. Jim listened intently, forcing himself not to smile, as they explained to him how they knew the murderer was a drifter/transient/drug user type. When they saw Brian Paige's picture on the news, he "looked like" a crazed madman.

Jim surmised that, on some level, we all need to believe we know something we don't really know, or that may not even be true or accurate. Bill and Ray seemed to derive comfort from the notion that they could find an individual who fit their profile of a murderer, then point at that guy and say, "that's the bad guy." He would be an unknown abstract idea, a psychopath or sociopath that existed on the fringes and periphery of society. Not a member of the mainstream. It was surely easier and safer than believing that a killer might lurk inside a lot of people, or that they may actually be in the presence of or be acquainted with a serial murderer. Jim didn't wish to destroy their fantasy and was glad when they moved off this subject and onto the next outrage that hit the front page.

Jim decided to lie down on his bed before heading out. He undressed down to his underwear and undershirt and got in bed on top of the covers, with his hands interlocked behind his head. While staring up at the ceiling, he replayed the events of the last 22 months in his head. It was almost as if he were going to die and his whole life was flashing before his eyes. Yet, his health was good, and he wasn't ready to give up on his future.

Although he had many regrets, he realized he couldn't change the past. If he dwelled on what he'd become, his mind would spiral into a state from which he feared he might never recover. His plan going forward was to take life one day at a time and make the best out of each one. Neither his past actions nor the death of his brother could be altered. Jim had allowed his hatred, bitterness, sadness and rage to engulf him, possess him and essentially change him into a monster. Somewhere, someday, he may have to answer for that. But the lesson he learned was that he must find a way to deal with the past and process it in a different manner. He also felt grateful that he wouldn't be spending the rest of his life behind bars. Although it came at a price, Detective Joe Devlin had provided him with not only freedom but a gateway to a fresh start in his life.

William Dunn had been very gracious when Jim went into his office a month or so ago to request a transfer to their San Francisco office. Dunn had contacted his counterpart and former law school classmate, Kimberly Coleman, who had met Jim before and was happy to have him as part of her team. Jim also felt he owed a courtesy good-bye to Douglas White. White looked up from his luxury car magazine long enough to say, "We wish you luck, John."

Between mid-October and the end of the year, Jim would have to wrap up his cases and provide a memo to Dunn about his outstanding files. A new attorney would be assigned to them. Jim would do his best to bring that individual up to speed, and that would be that. He figured on a good-bye dinner or two, maybe a going away party, and then he'd be on his way to the to the Golden State to begin work by the first week of the new year.

Jim had never lived anywhere but New York, so there was some trepidation about the move. He'd visited the San Francisco office a few times but hadn't gotten a chance to know anyone on any meaningful level. The only person he really would know in the entire state was Joe Devlin. Jim wondered if their paths would ever cross again. Speaking of Devlin…Jim sprung out of bed to get ready for his walk.

He finished tying the laces of his brand-new Nike sneakers. He had just treated himself last weekend. A Columbus Day sale at the mall. Basic black with gray trim. It was a little chilly tonight, so he chose black sweatpants rather than shorts. He finished off his outfit with a long sleeve Under Armour shirt and a black baseball cap. He would wear a black hooded sweatshirt also, as the cool night air required.

He went downstairs to get a bottle of water to bring with him. After using the bathroom, he kissed Anakin two times on top of his sturdy head and wolfed down a granola bar. Anakin gave Jim a stare, hoping he would be invited on the walk. But Jim assured the robust Rottweiler that tonight was not a good night for that, promising exercise over the weekend. Sensing he was not welcome on the walk, Anakin retired to his dog bed between the big screen TV and the fireplace.

Jim's thoughts turned to his neighbors two doors down. He took solace in the knowledge that he'd be supplying a going away present tonight. Almost one year ago, the Bradleys and the Devlins had shared a nice Thanksgiving together. They shared the bonds of family, great loss and tragedy.

Tonight, Jim planned to hold up his end of the bargain. When the news of the death of Keith Jenkins was eventually told to Devlin, the detective would then fulfill his obligation to Jim, and the matter would be finished. Emotionally, this entire episode in their lives would never truly conclude but executing the mechanics of their agreement was compulsory.

As harrowing as this ordeal had been, the fact that it would soon be over, and the hope that a new career and personal opportunities may be waiting for him in San Francisco, was beginning to provide Jim with some small measure of serenity. He needed to build on it, but it was a start. His parents would be up again for Thanksgiving next month, and Jim would be with them in Florida for the holidays. Maybe when his mom and dad saw him moving on with his life, they'd be able to achieve a modicum of tranquility.

The Devlins, too, were in need of peace. No parent should have to go through what they did. When Jim thought of their son's and his brother's deaths, it made him feel even guiltier about the 16 victims and their families. He couldn't dwell on that as it would paralyze him psychologically, and this wasn't the night for regrets. Tonight, the focus must be on the closure that he would be providing to Joe and Patty.

With all of the relevant information Detective Devlin had provided regarding the whereabouts and daily activities of Keith Jenkins committed to memory, Jim was ready to carry out his responsibility.

The ringing of the doorbell jolted Jim out of his thoughts and Anakin out of his bed. Jim opened the door to find his next-door-neighbor, Mrs. O'Connor, standing under the light. She was about 40 and thin, with a blonde ponytail and green eyes. She wore a Save the Elephants hooded sweatshirt and gray sweats.

"Hi, Sheila. What brings you out tonight?"

"Hi, Jim. Sorry to bother you. I'm returning your book. You were right, I really enjoyed it. This Nelson DeMille can really tell a story. Wow!"

"It's no bother, Sheila. I have most of his books upstairs, so if you ever want to borrow one, please don't hesitate to ask. But you didn't have to rush over here tonight to bring it back."

"We're going away for the weekend and I was afraid I would forget. Also, I wanted to give you my key, so you'd be able to water my plants. Tom's being a real pain in my you-know-what tonight, so I figured I'd get some space rather than making him wear my skillet."

Jim laughed. "Are you two love birds going 12 rounds again? You should kiss and make up."

"He can kiss my…Well, ok, you're right." She smirked. "We can get divorced after we come home from our weekend away. Goodnight Jim and enjoy the weekend. Thanks for taking care of my plants."

"Goodnight and have a good time."

Jim shut the door, chuckling at his interaction with Sheila O'Connor. They were good people, and a funny couple, forever fighting and joking about separating. He thought neither would last 10 minutes without the other. The O'Connors were always there when Jim needed them, so he gladly watered their plants whenever they took the kids away. That thought reminded Jim that in all her kidding around about her husband, Mrs. "O" had forgotten to give Jim her key. She must have remembered once she got home, because a few moments later the doorbell rang again.

Jim wiped his hands on a dishtowel, told Anakin to stay and moved toward the door hurriedly. His hope was that his neighbor was returning with her key, and without any of Tom's blood on her sweatshirt. He opened the door expecting to see Sheila O'Connor illuminated by his porch light, but instead was met by the raised jaw, flaring nostrils and cold, steel, piercing eyes of FBI Agent Russell Hollander.

About the Author

Louis Bruno grew up in New York with a love of family, sports, animals, crime novels, writing and storytelling. He moved to California in 2021. He's held positions in the legal field for over 20 years and currently works as a paralegal in an Oakland law firm.

His background includes a nonfiction work entitled *Life on the Periphery: An Ordinary Man's View of the World*, and two short stories written as a participant in the Gotham Writers Workshop.

His most profound happiness is spending time with his wife and daughters, as well as their Labrador Terrier four-legged son.